TO CROWN A KING

TO CROWN A KING

STEVEN J. JOHNSON

Northwest Publishing, Inc.
Salt Lake City, Utah

To Crown A King

For information address: Northwest Publishing, Inc.
6906 South 300 West, Salt Lake City, Utah 84047
B.K. 9-23-94
Edited by: S. Williams

PRINTING HISTORY
First Printing 1995

ISBN: 1-56901-479-5

NPI books are published by Northwest Publishing, Incorporated,
6906 South 300 West, Salt Lake City, Utah 84047.
The name "NPI" and the "NPI" logo are trademarks belonging to
Northwest Publishing, Incorporated.

PRINTED IN THE UNITED STATES OF AMERICA.
10 9 8 7 6 5 4 3 2 1

To Elissa:
Who makes every day I spend with her a
wonderful story-book tale.

Acknowledgments

Thanks to my parents, Don and Colleen, for their wonderful support, as well as Bill and Linda N. Thanks to Kris and Elissa for being my unofficial personal editors. Most of all, thanks to Art "imus" Przybilla, the wise old sage of my world, for caring enough to take the time to make a difference.

"LIKE FATHER, LIKE...?"

"Don't you think it's about time you get home, Sis? Go on—I'll finish up here and follow you," Ben remarked as he watched his sister move a box from one table to another close by.

"No," NeShae snapped back. "I told mother I'd stay here until the sun sets, and that's what I'm going to do. So go home, I'll be along in a few hours."

"Well, all right, but if you aren't back by supper time, I'm coming back to drag you home, understand?"

"Yes, my dear big brother," NeShae agreed sarcastically.

At that, Ben shrugged his shoulders helplessly and strolled off into the crowd of the busy marketplace. Ben was only a man of about twenty-five years, but he looked as though he had the wisdom of a hundred. His shiny black hair settled on

1

his shoulders, and his dark beard gave him the look of a much older man. He stood well over six feet tall and was very well built, which was the result of many long years of work on his father's farm.

He turned around and took one last look at his younger sister, who was now busy talking to a customer at her small stand. NeShae, he thought, was certainly a beautiful young lady. Some day, some man would be lucky. Her hair was a golden brown which reflected the sun's light, giving her a goddesslike appearance. She was tall for a woman, standing just a bit over five and a-half feet, and her slender, well-shaped body made more than one man turn to look while walking down the street.

He gave up his thoughts, however, and turned to make his way back home, since it was well over two miles through the woods. His father's farm lay just outside the city of Terrigrin, which was where NeShae went to set up her market stand once every month. Although the products she sold were not worth great amounts of money, she earned enough to buy the few things she wanted during the year. NeShae's products were original, though.

"Can I help you, sir?" NeShae started before she realized who she was talking to. "Oh, I'm sorry, my prince; I did not recognize you. Can I help you on this fine day?"

Prince Alexander Denmoore was the son of King Dlemar Denmoore, the mighty ruler of Terrigrin. King Dlemar had successfully opened the two trading routes out of Terrigrin which had allowed the city to prosper. The king had dealt with goblins, orcs, wolves, and invading tribesmen for many years in order to keep the trading routes open. He was well respected by those for miles around. His son, however, was a little different. Alexander placed pleasure before work. Not that he wasn't well trained in the arts of war and weapons, for he was. Perhaps it was just that he should have been forced to work more than he actually did, and for this, many labeled him a spoiled brat. Today he was at the market place looking for that little bit of excitement he just didn't get at the "boring old castle." At his side was his bodyguard and friend, Robin, who was also the king's wartime advisor. NeShae slowly eyed Alex, trying not to make it known that she was staring at him. He was a very handsome man, probably only three or four years older than she. His blond hair complemented him very well, with his well-toned body and striking clothes.

The prince smiled at her for a short moment, and then spoke, "Perhaps you can help me, my beautiful young lady. What is it you are selling here today?"

The compliment from the prince made NeShae's heart pound inside her, but she kept her composure and answered his question with confidence. "I sell not lamps, nor wine, nor weapons, but creations of beauty. I create sculptures of objects and animals from wood brought by caravans. Would you care to take a look, my prince?"

"If your sculptures are but half as beautiful as you, I will buy fifty. And please, call me Alex," the prince replied.

Surely all those stories about the prince being spoiled were wrong, NeShae thought to herself. This man was kind, courteous, and gentle, just as a prince should be.

"I will be right back, my pr...er, Alex." With that, she turned around to her small wagon and gently lifted from a box a number of small statues which she brought over to Alex.

Alex looked at the beautiful carvings and asked, "Did you carve all of these yourself?"

"Well, yes and no. You see, I made them, but I did not carve them," was her answer.

"What do you mean by that?"

"It was a gift I had when I was born. If I concentrate hard enough, the wood will bend and twist into a picture that I imagine for it."

Alex looked quite intrigued at this response, but saw no reason to press the issue any further. "As I said before, I will take fifty of your sculptures, for they are very beautiful indeed." At this he gave her a suggestive smile and looked to Robin, who had been standing very patiently until now. Robin understood the prince's glance and proceeded to pull out a bag of coins and hand them to Alex.

NeShae couldn't believe this! She hadn't sold fifty carvings in the last four months together! "At the moment," she began, awestruck, "I have only twenty carvings finished. However, I can finish the rest within two weeks."

Alex nodded his head in affirmation and handed her fifty silver coins. NeShae's hands almost started to tremble. She had never seen that much silver at one time in her entire life. Oh, how proud her parents would be!

"Thank you very much...Alexander," was all she could manage to spit out at that moment. She thought to herself, this man is not a spoiled child, but a servant of the gods!

"You're very welcome. Would you like me to help you pack up your stand?" the prince asked.

Before NeShae could even gladly say yes, she saw Alex turn his head sharply at the calling of his name. His father, King Dlemar, was walking briskly over to NeShae's stand. He stopped before the stand and looked slowly from Alex to Robin to NeShae. After a few moments, he finally spoke.

"Where have you been? Your lessons have long awaited you."

"But Father, there are many greater lessons to be learned right here on the street of this town," Alex started, trying to calm his father's anger enough to talk reasonably with him. "For example," he started to whisper, "take this lowly peasant girl. I have taught her that miracles can happen, even when dealing with ugly carvings!" At this he began to laugh ferociously. Little did he know that NeShae had heard every word.

"You will come with me. Now." Dlemar turned and walked away.

With no regret whatsoever, Alex shrugged his shoulders and turned to say good-bye to NeShae. The anger on her face, however, told him that she had overheard their conversation, every word of it.

"Let me make it up to you. Meet me here tonight in a few hours," he suggested.

But from the look on her face, he knew she wasn't going

to jump into his arms and say yes. "I would rather walk the Abyss for a dwarf's lifetime than be anywhere with you for one lousy minute!" she shouted out loud. "I'll have your carvings done in two weeks. That is, if you still want these 'ugly carvings.'" She stomped away as tear after tear rolled down her face. Yes, she thought, the rumors were true after all.

At this scene the prince looked at Robin, rolled his eyes, and responded jokingly, "Women." With only a hint of a smile on his face, he told Robin they should probably head back to the castle before the king became too upset. Robin agreed totally, and they were gone as quickly as they had come. The only thing they left behind was a sobbing young girl with much pride, who swore she would get even with this stuck-up prince.

After a few minutes of crying, NeShae finally decided to start packing up her carvings so she could make her way home in time for supper. She placed everything neatly into her donkey-drawn cart and slowly made her way down the trail, homeward bound. By the time she pulled into the little farm that she called home, the sun had already begun to set, and she was sure that supper would be done. She quickly led the donkey to the stables and put her beloved carvings in a designated spot in the barn. Then she made her way into the large white building that had provided the comfort of home to her all of the nineteen years of her life. She found that supper was almost ready when she walked in, as her father and brother were at the table discussing something, while her mother was getting ready to serve.

"What kept you so long, NeShae?" her father asked as soon as she walked through the door. Although he was a man of about sixty years, he was still very much the head of the household, and always had the final say in matters.

"I was at the market with my carvings," she responded, not looking at her father face to face.

"But why did you stay so late tonight?" he asked again.

"I was talking to the prince," she blurted out before she even had a chance to think what she was saying.

"The prince!" Ben said as he stood up. "Why in the gods' creations would you want to talk to that overgrown child? Did he bother you? If he did, I want to know. It's about time somebody changes his attitude about all of us 'little people' around him."

"What was he like, dear?" questioned NeShae's mother, who had been quiet until now.

"Well," NeShae began, "All the rumors about him being a spoiled brat are true. But I think he really does have a good side to him. If only someone could get at it."

"I could get at it quite easily, and willingly," Ben growled as he shook his head and made a threatening fist.

"Enough of this talk," their father said at once. "We have food to eat, and an evening to enjoy." Indeed they did.

"But Father, I only went to the marketplace for a little excitement. This old castle gets a little boring at times, you know," said Alex.

"That's no excuse to neglect your duties. I've given you enough chances, Alex. Maybe it's time to do something a little more drastic," his father said sternly.

"More drastic? What do you mean by that?" the prince asked in a somewhat worried voice.

"I mean I think it's time you were sent to live with Artimus for a while. Maybe he can teach you a little respect and discipline. I know I've tried, but you just don't understand. If you're going to be king someday, you have to grow up. And you don't seem to be growing up here. That is my decision. You will leave tomorrow morning, so be ready."

After his speech, King Dlemar left Alex alone in the dining chamber to ponder what had just happened. To live with Artimus? Is he crazy? That man is nothing but a senile old fool, he thought to himself. Maybe it's just a threat, he reasoned, and maybe he'll forget about the whole thing by tomorrow morning. Hopefully.

Morning came quickly for Alex, for a guard woke him at

dawn. "I have been sent here to tell you that arrangements with Artimus have been made, and that you are to go there this morning. Your horse is waiting in the stables, and you are to leave as soon as you are done with breakfast."

Alex couldn't believe it. His father was actually going through with this. Hopefully it wouldn't last for more than a week or two, though. He couldn't possibly put up with that old coot's mumbling for long. He chose to follow his father's bidding, however, so he quickly got dressed and went down to breakfast. Surprisingly, King Dlemar wasn't there to join him as he usually was. Maybe he had some business. Or maybe he was just too upset even to join his only son at breakfast, Alex thought to himself. As soon as he was done eating, he went up to his room to get some extra clothes and his sword. Then he made his way slowly to the stables. "I had better get this over with," he murmured under his breath.

Artimus lived only a few miles out of Terrigrin, with no one around except for a couple of small farms in the area. As Alex rode, he thought of all the stories he had heard about the famous Artimus. It was said that in his younger days, he was an assassin, a trained killer who had more than perfected his art. The stories said that he was feared in the realms for hundreds of miles around, for he was Artimus the Black, a silent killer hired by the highest bidder. After a number of years, however, Artimus simply vanished. No one heard of him for years, until he showed up just outside of Terrigrin. Of course, everyone in the city was terrified of the man, but he soon earned their trust, and never seemed to bother anyone or become hostile again. So he lived in peace. His reputation as a fighter was not lost though, and because of this, King Dlemar and Artimus became very good friends, even sharing moments of battle together. That is how, Alex was sure, he had become stuck in this nightmare. Artimus was doing this as a favor to his father.

He reached Artimus's tiny hut in a very short time and began to look the place over. His house was very small, indeed, and was placed right in the center of a small patch of woods, which gave him the shelter and privacy he evidently longed for. He wearily approached and dismounted. Alex tied his horse to a small tree and walked confidently to the front door. He didn't even have time to flinch before he felt a dagger at his throat.

"Your skills are very poor indeed. Your father was right," came a voice behind him, which obviously belonged to the person holding the dagger. The dagger was released, and Alex immediately spun around to meet the person who so dared to challenge him, the prince. Before him he saw a wondrous sight: a figure in a dark purple robe, but not a human. It was an elf! An elf with long gray flowing hair with a hint of silver at its ends, and yellow eyes that seemed to see right through Alex.

Without another thought, Alex reached for the sword by his side, but almost fell over when he grabbed only air.

"Looking for this?" the elf chuckled, holding Alex's sword out to him.

"I take it you're Artimus," Alex said, glaring at the man in front of him, while at the same time taking his sword.

"Well, yes, indeed I am, young prince. And you have much to learn. Much to learn, indeed."

NeShae had gotten up early that morning, for there was a caravan arriving early in town, and she needed much wood for the many carvings she had left to finish. NeShae quickly did her morning chores, ate a small breakfast, and set off for town on her horse. Yes, the prince had upset her tremendously, but a deal was a deal, and she would have those carvings done for him as promised.

As she passed the small thicket of woods to her left, she saw her silver-haired friend outside that morning. Many dawns she had walked right past him, only to turn and see Artimus staring into the morning sunlight with a small smile on his face. She wondered what he was thinking then. But it didn't matter, for he had become a very good friend of her family, and he was a good person, no matter what others thought. The past, NeShae thought to herself, is just that—past.

She looked more closely this morning, however, for there seemed to be another figure in the trees with Artimus. She couldn't quite make out who it was, but it made her curious, for Artimus had very few visitors. She looked again, but couldn't see well enough to identify the other figure. "I guess it's none of my business anyway," she told herself as she continued down the road to Terrigrin to get her precious wood.

"You want me to what?" Alex cried, almost dumbfounded. Today was the second day they had been together, and most of the day before had been spent getting to know the place. Besides, Artimus had gone to Terrigrin to tend to some business and had left Alex there all alone.

"I want you to strike me with your sword," Artimus explained again in his same calm tone.

Alex was confused. Did this crazy old elf want to die so badly that he would have someone stab him?

"Just do it!" Artimus said powerfully with a hint of finality in his voice.

He didn't know why, but he felt like he had to obey his crazy host. So he reluctantly, but quickly, moved his sword above his head for the strike against his unarmed foe. Before he even knew what hit him, the seemingly fragile old elf grabbed Alex's sword hand and twisted it. At the same time, he brought one leg behind Alex, and pushed him to the ground. In the blink of an eye, Alex was on his back looking up at Artimus. He could feel the gentle touch of a sword on his neck, and knew it to be his own, the one he had held so firmly only seconds ago.

"Your first lesson; heed it well. Never underestimate any foe. It could easily spell your death, as it would have now," Artimus said quietly, but sternly. "That is enough for today. Now go fetch us some water from the well."

He lay the sword on Alex's chest and walked slowly into the house, admiring the trees and beauty around him as he went. Alex was shocked. He had never seem a man or elf move that fast. And Artimus's words made sense to Alex. They made a lot of sense. Maybe this old elf wasn't quite as crazy as he had thought. Maybe he could learn something from him after all.

Artimus slowly closed the door and walked over to the small window on the other side of the room. Sitting on the edge was one of his closest friends, Ptilon, a great falcon with whom he shared his thoughts and innermost feelings.

"He has so much to learn, my dear friend," Artimus said dryly as he put a hand on the falcon's head. "And little does he know of the great perils that stand in front of him."

"THE ROOT OF ALL..."

Galdon stared at his crystal ball, hoping and wishing he could find some weakness in the king's defenses. He had been studying the Castle of Terrigrin for weeks now in preparation for the day he would begin his masterful plan. There was a knock on the door to his dark shadowy room at that moment, which caused him to lose his concentration. His scrying sphere went black and Galdon looked to the door in vengeful anger. Who dared interrupt him? Galdon slowly opened the door to see a guard who was apparently bringing a message. The guard's face turned white when he saw the evil grin on Galdon's face, but he didn't make any move to leave.

"I have news, Your Greatness," the pale guard said hesitantly.

"Speak," was all Galdon replied.

"We did as you asked," the guard continued. "We have the sacred artifact in a secure place in the lower chambers of your tower. There will be guards posted there at all times."

Galdon turned around so that his back was to the guard and whispered, "Good. Very good. And one last thing," Galdon said, turning once again to face the guard. "Never disturb me while I'm working."

The last thing the frightened guard saw was a shiny dagger entering his chest. Then he knew no more. As the body sank to the floor, Galdon looked at the blank face and said one more time in a cold harsh voice, "Never."

"You want me to what?" Alex said for the third time today. Artimus had grown tired of him asking this when he was told to do something, but explained it to him again.

"I want you to try to strike me," was Artimus's only reply.

"But you're blindfolded!" Alex snapped back in a bewildered tone.

"That I am. Now do as you are told," Artimus growled.

At first Alex didn't like the idea of striking a blind man, but then he remembered Artimus's earlier words, "Never underestimate a foe." Alex grabbed the sword from his side and raised it to strike his teacher. As his weapon started its downward motion, however, it was met by another sword just inches from Artimus's head, the elf's sword. Alex swung again, and then again, thinking it was impossible for this to be happening. But every time, the agile elf's sword was waiting to parry each harmless blow.

After a few moments, Alex stopped and looked at Artimus. With awe in his eyes, he whispered to himself, "I bet you were once unstoppable."

Artimus removed his blindfold and threw it to Alex, saying, "Now it's your turn."

Alex gave him a joking look and said, "No thanks. I prefer to keep my neck."

"Put it on," Artimus said sternly, his patience growing weak from the prince's attitude. "Please put it on," he said again, this time in a much calmer tone.

Alex reluctantly put the piece of cloth around his head and tied it. "Now what am I supposed to do? Wait to die?" Alex asked as he held his sword at his side.

Artimus's voice said calmly, "Concentrate, my young prince. Focus all of your emotions on your opponent—think as he would think."

Alex tried, but as soon as Artimus stopped speaking, he felt the flat of a sword gently slap his cheek. Then again, and again.

"I can't do this!" Alex screamed, as he swung his sword wildly.

"Use your anger," Artimus continued. "Focus all of your anger, joy, sorrow, and frustration on your foe. Become one with your opponent."

Alex was beginning to understand now. He stopped swinging his sword wildly and began concentrating on Artimus. He tried to picture what Artimus would do and focused every emotion he was feeling into stopping that one blow. In one fluid motion, Alex raised his sword in an attempt to parry any blows that might be aimed at his head. Just as he positioned his sword, he heard the clang of metal on metal, and felt his arms jerk back.

"I did it!" he yelled as he threw off the blindfold. "I parried a strike from your sword!" The prince, happy beyond belief, almost began dancing, but he knew that Artimus was still watching him. With a triumphant smile on his face, he turned again to look at the elf.

"Indeed you did," was his only reply. Artimus could barely contain his smile, however, as he turned and walked to the house. The prince was improving faster than he had expected.

NeShae had gotten up early that morning so she could continue working on her carvings. It had been a week and a half since she had talked to the prince, and she only had three carvings left to finish. She was going to be done earlier than expected. Maybe she could even deliver the carvings this evening. Just as she was about to start working again, she heard the sound of hooves as a horse rode up to the barn. On its back was a young boy dressed as a messenger, holding the flag of Terrigrin, a white ax connecting two roads on a black background. This symbolized King Dlemar's success in driving out all of their enemies and opening the trade routes. NeShae slowly exited the barn and asked the young boy what his business was.

"I am here to tell Mr. Benjamin Neerith that he is again needed in the royal ranks of the king's Guard. He is to come immediately," the messenger explained.

"But…" NeShae was cut off before she could even begin to protest.

"Let me get my gear, and I'll be right with you," said a voice behind them. It was Ben's voice.

NeShae spun around to face her older brother. "But Ben, you can't go. You've already spent two years in that army. You've done your time. Stay here with Mom and Dad, and me. Please."

Ben leaned toward her and kissed her on the forehead. "You know I can't do that, Sis. It's my duty. Besides, I'll be back before you know it."

Ben turned and went to the house to get a few of his possessions. NeShae thought about Ben's previous experiences with the king's army. He had gone in when he was only twenty-one, had served for two years, and had fought in three major trade route wars. He had been lucky, for he had come home. Maybe he wouldn't be so lucky this time.

NeShae shrugged that awful thought off and thought back to when Ben had been promoted to the king's Guard just one year after entering the army. The king's Guard was the highest honor attainable in the army, and many people were proud of Ben for that achievement, including NeShae. She still didn't want him to go, but she knew there was no way she could stop him. Then she wondered to herself, why did the king need Ben? Was another war in the making? She had to satisfy both her curiosity and concern, so she asked the messenger.

"Lately there have been many goblin and orc tribes wandering the routes," the messenger responded. "Extra protection for trade caravans is needed, so the regular guards from the castle have been moved to the trade routes. The king's Guard has been called to protect the castle, should any enemies happen to try something."

A few moments later Ben appeared again, walking toward NeShae and the messenger boy. He had a pack on his shoulder, which looked full. He also wore the designated suit of platemail armor, given only to members of the king's Guard. The entire set of armor, his shield and his shining sword were all colored perfectly in black and white. Ben was quite a sight at this moment, NeShae thought with tears forming in her eyes. Yes, she was proud of him, but she was also scared. Very scared.

Ben went to get his horse, and a few minutes later appeared on a white mount. He rode up to NeShae, looked down at her and spoke softly, "Don't worry, Sis. I'll be fine. Tell Mom and Dad when they get back from town that I'll be back before they know it." Ben turned to ride away, but then stopped and gave one final look to NeShae and said, "I love you, Sis." Then he and the messenger rode off into the morning haze.

NeShae, with her eyes full of tears, could only stare as her big brother rode off. Quietly she said to herself, "I love you too, Ben."

Galdon eyed the crystal ball again. His plan was working perfectly. "Guard!" he shouted suddenly. "Get me Larrin!"

In a few moments, an enormous warrior stepped through the doorway and into the room. "You called, Master?" the deep voice asked. The man was huge, standing at least seven feet tall, and looked as though he could crush a man with his fingers.

"Get your troops ready. We move in two weeks. Those goblin tribes have thinned out the castle guards enough for us to begin," Galdon said.

Larrin pondered the thought for a while, then spoke. "Yes, but haven't the king's Guards arrived by now?"

"Of course, you idiot," Galdon snapped. "But there are many fewer of them, and with my magic, they don't stand a chance. In two weeks the precious king will be mine. And with the Crown of Vallchem, soon the entire city and its trade routes will be mine also!" All that followed was a cold, ghostly laugh.

NeShae had finished all her carvings that day and had told her parents of Ben's return to the king's Guard. They seemed less worried than she, for they knew that Ben was a very capable soldier. She went to bed early that evening and dreamed of horrible creatures battling the king's Guard, and winning. She awoke the next morning and packed her cart with the carvings she had been working on for over a week and a half. She started off to Terrigrin to deliver them to her ungrateful buyer, Prince Alexander. When she arrived, however, she was stunned to learn that he was staying with Artimus. Why was that child staying with her dear friend Artimus? It didn't matter. She would go there instead to deliver the goods.

It was still morning when she arrived at Artimus's doorstep. What was in front of her almost made her burst into laughter. On the ground, doing push-ups, was Prince Alex. And sitting on Alex's bare back was Artimus, legs crossed, with a smile on his face. Alex heard NeShae approach and looked up to meet her with an angry stare. She turned to Artimus and returned his smile. Alex sank to the ground, hoping that his morning training was now finished.

Artimus thought otherwise, though. "Did I tell you to stop?" came a reply from on top of Alex's back. The prince didn't even argue, for he knew that it got him nowhere. He reluctantly began the exercises again.

Artimus eyed NeShae and spoke, "May I help you, my young Lady?"

"Thank you, Artimus, but I am here to deal with your newfound childish student. I have some carvings which he bought from me a while back, and I am here to deliver them."

Artimus spoke again, "Well, that's fine, but you know the rules. Any guest of Artimus must stay for dinner." NeShae was very familiar with his rules and knew that it was pointless to argue, so she agreed. As soon as she did, Alex increased his pace without warning, so that Artimus nearly fell off his back. Artimus only smiled and looked to NeShae. "Agreed. Let's eat."

NeShae tied her donkey to a nearby tree and looked to Alex, who had been allowed to stop. "Are these 'ugly carvings' satisfactory, my prince?" she said with a great deal of sarcasm.

"Of course," he said shamefully. "But they are not ugly…"

"Don't say it. I've heard enough lies from you," she said as she piled the carvings carefully onto Artimus's porch. "There," she spoke when she was finished. "The deal's done."

Artimus looked at the two humorously. NeShae certainly was a fiery young woman. She reminded him of someone he once knew, long ago.

"Alex, go get some wood for the stove and prepare the food that's in the kitchen," Artimus said.

"But…" was all Alex could get out before the elf's eyes cut through him like a dagger. "Whatever you say," he finished, and walked off to do as he was told.

NeShae and Artimus stayed outside and talked as dinner was being prepared.

"Why is the prince staying with you, dear friend?" NeShae began.

"As a favor to the king," Artimus answered, although NeShae had hoped for more of an explanation.

"We met at the marketplace some time ago," NeShae continued.

"I know," said Artimus, "Ptilon was watching as you and Alex exchanged words. He told me all about it, for we communicate well without words."

"Why must he be so pig-headed?" NeShae asked.

"Because he knows no better. He has grown up thinking

that he can do nothing wrong, but he has learned much already. He may even make a fine man someday," Artimus said with a wink. "Now let's go have some dinner. Our servant should almost be done." At that they both laughed and walked into the cottage.

When they entered the small building, they saw that the table had been set, and that steaming bowls of food were sitting temptingly on the table. Alex was standing in front of the wood burning stove with his arms crossed and a towel flung over his left shoulder. As the two companions entered the room, Alex smiled and spoke, "Dinner is served, my masters." He then took a low bow and looked at NeShae and Artimus as all three of them burst into laughter. When dinner was finished, the three sat back and exchanged stories for a good part of the afternoon. It even seemed as though NeShae and Alex were getting along, for every time their eyes met each other, it was like the world had stopped around them.

Artimus told of his many adventures around the Realms, which excited both NeShae and Alex, for both of them longed for a little excitement in their dull lives. He told them of the many sights he had seen and of the dangers he had overcome. This struck a bit of curiosity into NeShae, and before she could stop herself, she asked, "Artimus, what did you do when you were younger? I mean…all of those rumors about you…"

"Being an assassin?" Artimus finished.

"Yes. Certainly that isn't true," NeShae said, confident that she was right.

"Well," continued Artimus, "an assassin means different things to different people. Yes, NeShae, I've killed too much in my life, but never was I paid for it, nor did I want to be. It was something I had to do." At the finish of his last statement, Artimus's eyes became fixed on the table as he got a starry look on his face, as though he was remembering some awful event from his secret past.

NeShae broke the silence and said, "I had better get home. Supper will be ready in only a few hours, and my chores await me."

Alex looked at her with a boyish gleam in his eyes and sheepishly asked, "Would you like me to ride with you until you reach your farm?"

NeShae only smiled and said in a teasing tone, "But my dear Prince, I am only a lowly peasant girl. I couldn't expect you to associate with the likes of me."

Alex cowardly looked at the floor for any hole that might be there for him to crawl into. Then he looked back into NeShae's beautiful green eyes and said in the most serious tone he had ever used, "I'm sorry."

NeShae started to soften, but then remembered the charade she was playing and spoke, "But Alex, you must continue your training and build your muscles. You don't have time for someone as unimportant as me." As she spoke of building muscles, NeShae put a hand on one of the prince's large biceps and gave it a joking squeeze. When she finished speaking, she gave Artimus a wink, thanked him for the dinner, and headed for the door.

She stopped and turned around as she heard the prince say, "Thank you for the carvings."

NeShae answered sarcastically, "It's the least I can do for someone as great as you." She chuckled softly and continued out the doorway to make her way home.

The whole time Artimus just sat back quietly shaking his head and laughing. The prince, still thinking of his conversation with NeShae, shook his head and smiled, "I wanted to stay here tonight anyway." He and Artimus looked at each other and laughed.

For the next two weeks, Artimus and Alex trained hard. Alex didn't understand why the elf was pushing him so hard, but he didn't question him. Besides, he had learned so much in the month that Artimus had been his teacher, that he wasn't sure if he wanted to go home. He knew that soon he would have to, though. He wanted to see his father, but he was tired of the fighting. Every day, it seemed, they would argue about something, usually dealing with the prince's attitude or the neglect of his duties. Maybe it was time to be the prince his father wanted, maybe he was finally ready.

His thoughts were disturbed by Artimus's voice as they prepared to continue Alex's sword training, "Strength is good, but quickness will win a battle nine times out of ten. Quickness is important, as is pride. Some opponents gloat, and sometimes they do it too soon, which can spell their death. If an opponent thinks you are dead, perhaps it will give you an advantage. Then again, perhaps he will finish you off when he has the chance."

Within seconds of his lecture, the clang of metal rang out over the nearby land. Every morning for the last month Alex and Artimus had performed this same exercise. At first, Alex lasted only a few seconds before Artimus gently touched him with his sword. But lately, Alex had grown into a much worthier opponent. The speed of the two figures was incredible, each matching the other's blow with a perfect parry. It seemed as though they were only two shadows doing battle in the morning light. The teacher and pupil continued for a number of minutes, which started to tire both of them, until suddenly, Alex dropped to the ground and grabbed his leg. "My knee!" he shouted as he rolled on the grass.

Alex was hoping that his faked injury would drop Artimus's guard, but when he felt the elf's sword gently touch his neck, he knew that his plan had miserably failed. Artimus just looked at him and smiled, "Nice try, but next time save it for a creature of less intelligence, perhaps a rock or tree." They both laughed wildly about Artimus's comment before they again started Alex's lessons.

They continued their training again after dinner, focusing on the long bow and dagger. Alex had gone through training at the Castle, but nothing like Artimus's teachings. At his home, he was taught to walk straight up to a man and try to defeat him by brute strength. Artimus had taught him the advantage of being very quick and agile. Alex felt confident with his newly built strength and quickness and the more he learned, the more he realized that he knew very little.

Alex's strength in weapons was with his sword, but he was also very skilled (thanks to Artimus) in the long bow and dagger. He also had a little training with a battle ax, but was certainly not proficient in its use.

Later that night, after supper, Alex and Artimus went outside and sat under the stars in the quietness of the dark evening. They had become very good friends in the last month, something that Alex had known little about before he met Artimus. They had both given each other something very important, for Alex had given the elf companionship, something that Artimus had longed for on many of these same starry nights. Artimus, on the other hand, had given the prince a new perspective on life. He had taught him to look deeper than the skin and clothes, and that being a Prince doesn't mean you're better, and in some cases, even means you're worse. Alex had grown more in the last month than in all of his twenty-one years of life put together. He owed Artimus much.

"Why do you live here like this?" Alex asked, breaking the silence.

"Like what?" the elf said dryly. "All alone? Not wanting to deal with the outside world? Because people do not accept elven 'assassins' with open arms, and I care not to prove myself to anyone."

"But surely I can help," the prince insisted. "I can tell everyone in the city how wise and strong you are. You will be accepted happily by the people, or they will die by my sword."

"Easy, O' Great Killing Machine," Artimus laughed, "for the people like a liar even less."

Alex chuckled at this statement, too, and fully understood the elf's motives. He would easily be accepted in most cities, but he chose this spot to be away from people because he wanted to. Not because he had to.

There was silence for a while, and then Alex spoke again, "Do you think NeShae really hates me?"

"Well, you didn't exactly impress her when you first met. But no, I don't think she hates you," Artimus reassured him.

"She's quite a lady," Alex said as they both stared up into

the star-filled horizon. A few moments later, Alex looked at Artimus and spoke, "I'd like to thank you, Artimus. You've opened my eyes like no one else could have. You've taught me so much. How can I ever repay you?"

"I'm sure I can think of something," Artimus said with a grin. He knew that if Alex was to survive in the future, he was going to need every bit of training he could find. Artimus just hoped he had taught him enough.

King Dlemar sat in his throne room along with his long-time wife and Alex's mother, Queen Andrea Denmoore. There were numerous Guards stationed around the room, including Ben, who had been on guard duty since after supper. Dlemar and Andrea were discussing Alex and whether they should send for him to come home or not. As they were talking, one of the king's Guards approached Dlemar and said, "Your Majesty, a young boy is here to see you. He says he brings important news."

"It's very late," The king replied, looking to the guard. "But send him in if it's so important."

"What do you think he wants?" Andrea asked Dlemar as soon as the Guard left to get the boy.

"I'm not sure," the king said softly as he tried to come up with the answer himself.

A short time later, the door to the throne room opened and a young dirty-looking lad walked in, escorted by two Guards.

"What brings you here, young man?" said the king in a fatherly tone.

"I bear great news," said the child.

"Then speak."

"I am here to tell you of a kingdom very close to here that desperately needs your help. It seems as though their King was captured by an evil mage," the boy started.

"What kingdom?" Dlemar asked suspiciously, for he had not heard of this news before.

"I believe it started with a T. Yes, let me think for a moment," the boy continued. "It was Temmer...no,

Terrer…no, Terrin…no, Terrigrin! That's it, Terrigrin!" The boy's face lit up and he began to laugh out loud. A cold, evil sounding laugh.

The Guards looked nervously at each other and put their hands on their swords. the king, with an outraged look on his face stood up and yelled, "Get this young prankster out of my sight!"

At the same time, the throne room doors burst open and a horde of orcs and goblins burst in, all swinging blackened swords. The king's Guard was filled with very experienced fighters, however, and stood their ground, until they realized that these swords were slicing through their weapons and armor as though they weren't even there. But the king's Guard had taken a vow: To defend the Royal family or die trying. And many of them did the latter.

During all of this commotion, the young boy who had entered the throne room had transformed into an older black-haired man in a long green robe. It was Galdon. He started chanting some arcane words, and in the blink of an eye, both he and King Dlemar were gone. Vanished.

As soon as the goblins and orcs saw this, they slowly backed off and made their way out of the Castle. Those monsters that were left, that is, for even though the evil beings had magical weapons and greatly outnumbered their foes, the king's Guard fought ferociously and made many of the monsters pay dearly for their intrusion. But the Guards had also paid dearly, for only six of twenty were left unharmed.

Ben lay on the floor trying to catch his breath as he looked at the bloody scene around him. The Queen, who had managed to stay clear of the enemies, became hysterical as one of the Guards tried to calm her. Others from the Castle who had heard the excitement came rushing in from all over in an effort to help the wounded in any way they could. Then Ben looked down and realized why he was lying on the floor. Stretching from his right shoulder to the opposite side of his waist was a large gaping wound which was spilling blood unto the floor. Ben felt uneasy at the sight, and then slipped into blackness.

Ptilon the falcon circled over the house of Artimus in the blackness of the night and slowly made his way to the window he had grown to know so well. Inside he saw his friend of many years sitting there in the darkness watching his small fire dance in his fireplace. Artimus sensed the falcon's presence and went over to the window.

"What is it, my friend?" asked Artimus.

In a way only the elf could understand, Ptilon told Artimus the entire story of what he had seen at the Castle. He told him of the king being captured.

Artimus looked at the floor wearily and sighed. Why did this have to happen so soon? "Thank you, Ptilon," the elf slowly replied, "I owe you much."

He walked back to his chair and sat again by the fireplace. "The time has come, Alexander," he whispered to himself. "I hope I have prepared you well."

"TREASURES OF THE HEART"

Alex awoke the next morning and sleepily wandered into the kitchen to find something to eat for breakfast. As he looked around the tiny cottage through his bleary eyes, he saw Artimus sitting in his chair staring at a fire that had been reduced to coals hours ago. Alex had left him there the night before going to bed, but surely he hadn't stayed there this whole time, he thought.

The prince approached Artimus, put a hand on his shoulder, and asked, "Are you all right?"

The elf slowly looked up at Alex with his usually fiery eyes. This time, however, his eyes were dull and saddened as though something terrible had happened. "It's your father. He's been captured," Artimus murmured softly.

Alex didn't know if he should laugh at the elf's cruel joke

or take him seriously. A sick feeling came over him and he didn't know what to say. All he could do was slowly lower himself into a chair that was sitting next to Artimus.

"What do you mean, my father has been captured?" Alex questioned in a dazed tone.

Artimus told Alex the entire story, as Ptilon had told him the night before. After the shock on Alex's face wore off, and he was able to speak again, he finally asked, "Well, what's being done about it? Who has been sent after him?"

Artimus slowly shook his head and said, "No one."

"What?" the prince screamed in anger. "Not one person? Why not?"

"Because most of the king's Guard was killed during the battle, and to send out a hundred troops would be like telling the king's captor what time they'd be arriving. Besides, no one knows where he's been taken."

"Well, something has to be done. I'll go find my father myself if I have to," Alex growled in a frustrated voice. "How can I find out where he's been taken?"

"Calm down," Artimus said slowly. "If you are going to rescue your father, time is critical. This mage must have a purpose for the king...you must find him soon. You must start tomorrow by going to Donaville, a week and a half's travel from here. There you will find a sage named Merquill who can help. I'll help you start packing right now."

Alex was hardly listening, for he was thinking of how he was going to destroy this evil mage who had dared to interfere with his family. He would have his revenge.

"Where are Mother and Father?" Ben asked in more of a painful groan than a voice.

"They will be here anytime," NeShae answered. "For now, just rest."

She kissed Ben on the cheek and watched as he slowly closed his eyes. She held his hand in silence for a few moments before she rose to exit the room. Outside the door she met one of the clerics who had tried to heal Ben. She nervously asked him if Ben were going to be all right.

"I'm afraid I can't be sure," the cleric responded, "for his wounds are magical, not natural. There's not much more we can do for him without examining the weapon that wounded him, and there were none left after the battle."

"But there must be something we can do," NeShae pleaded.

"I'm afraid that without one of those weapons, your brother stands little chance of survival," the cleric spoke quietly. Then he told her what they looked like, from the description given to him by one of the other surviving guards. "The weapons are long swords, covered entirely in black," he continued, "and the guard said he could remember a large letter G engraved on the blades in gold writing."

"You mean if I bring back one of those magical weapons, my brother could be cured?" NeShae asked with a glimmer of hope in her voice.

"He and five others who were wounded in the same way," the cleric answered. "But it must be done quickly, for he will not stay healthy for more than three or four more months. By then the magic of the wound will have taken over his body."

"Then keep him well as long as you can," NeShae responded, as she turned and sprinted out of the castle. She almost ran into her parents as she turned a corner to make her way to the stables to get her horse.

"Is he all right?" NeShae's mother asked her frantically.

"Not right now, but he may be soon. I love you both." At that, NeShae turned and ran to the stables. She had to go to Artimus to get his help, "If ever you had an answer, my friend, please let it be now."

King Dlemar was finally sitting in front of the man who was responsible for his kidnapping. He looked him over carefully, searching for any weakness that might prove to be helpful in the future. The man standing in front of the king was quite short, obviously not any great warrior, and was wearing a long robe decorated with many different-colored stripes on a black background. His forehead was long and his gray beard nearly reached the bottom of his neck. He stood hunched over with a dark brown staff held in his right hand, looking at the king, waiting for a response.

"What do you want with me, you cowardly, stinkin' wizard?" Dlemar screamed at Galdon.

"Hush, hush," came the mage's reply. "You mustn't get angry, my dear king, for we must start the planning of our great empire together. It's going to be wonderful, don't you think, Kingy? I'll be able to rule everything through you as soon as the Crown takes effect. No one will suspect a thing, will they, Kingy?" Galdon followed his speech with long shrill laughter that echoed through the hallways of his evil domain.

Alex paced nervously back and forth in front of the cottage as Artimus watched occasionally from a window. Then Alex heard something, the sound of hooves coming his way. In the blink of an eye, he grabbed his sword and ducked behind a set of small bushes. The only forested area for miles on the plains around Terrigrin was here around Artimus's house, so Alex could clearly see the lone rider approaching rapidly. He stayed behind his cover until Artimus appeared from inside his hut and stated in a dull voice, "NeShae approaches."

As the rider got closer, Alex could see that the rider was indeed NeShae. But what was she doing here now? NeShae rode directly up to Artimus, almost ignoring Alex, and desperately spit out the words, "My brother has been wounded and the king was captured and…" She tried to catch her breath as she slid off her horse.

"We know, my dear. Ptilon came to me last night," Artimus said painfully.

NeShae told both Artimus and Alex the story about her brother and her need to find one of the magical weapons that had wounded him. After she was finished, Artimus relayed his story about the king's disappearance, as his falcon companion had told him. When he was done, the three of them sat there in silence for what seemed like centuries, until NeShae could no longer keep quiet and asked Artimus, "What can I do? I must get that weapon before it's too late."

"And I must save my father," Alex added.

Artimus looked from the young confident warrior to the beautiful craftswoman and said, "It looks as though you have answered each other's questions."

"Put it on!" Galdon screamed at the top of his lungs as he held an object in front of the disobedient king. It was the Crown. It was gold in color with rich jewels of various sorts outlining it, the largest being an enormous emerald set in the very front. "You will do as you are told." Then he paused for a moment and started again, "Larrin, will you kindly show our friend here what happens when my servants do not obey?"

Without one hint of emotion, the bulging warrior strolled over to the chair where the king's hands were tied behind his back. Larrin arrived there just in time to feel a sharp pain as a foot slammed into his groin. the king only smiled as he retracted his leg and looked to the mage. As Larrin doubled over in pain, Galdon's only comment was, "This may take longer than expected."

"You want us to go together?" NeShae asked unbelievingly. "How can I expect to find that weapon if I'm tagging along behind Mr. Macho looking for his father?"

"We'll find the weapon first," said Alex, who had been quiet up until now.

Both Artimus and NeShae looked at the prince in amazement. Did they hear him right? That spoiled prince was actually thinking of someone else instead of himself?

NeShae, almost too shocked to catch her breath, said wonderingly, "What? You want to go help me find that weapon while your father, the king, waits who-knows-where to be rescued? Are you catching a fever?" Even though NeShae acted a little hostile to the prince, deep down her respect for Alex swelled at his last statement. Artimus had been a miracle worker with him.

Artimus spoke again, "Perhaps you don't need to choose

one quest over the other. It would only make sense that both of your goals lie in the same place, wherever that is." Then he told them both of the sage in Donaville again, for he wasn't sure how much Alex had heard the first time. When he had finished, Alex and NeShae eyed each other expectantly until Alex finally spoke, "It looks as though we will be traveling together."

"Indeed it does," NeShae replied as she stared at Alex with hope in her eyes and a small smile on her face, the first smile she had worn all day.

For the rest of the afternoon, Artimus told them of the things and people they should expect on the way to Donaville. Alex had been there a few times before, but to NeShae it would be a totally new experience. Artimus helped them finish packing their things, gave them supper, and then sent them to bed early, knowing that many evil things awaited them. All slept well that night except for Artimus, who was searching through old trunks, looking for items he had put away many years ago.

"You're trying my patience, Kingy," Galdon frustratedly told his captive. "But no matter. You cannot refuse the Crown forever. You see, its magic is already starting to work on you. Soon you will not be able to resist it, my king. And then it will control your mind. Or rather I will control your mind through it. Soon all of your needless hostility toward me will be gone. In fact, soon we will be looking over the city of Terrigrin together, the city that I will rule. With your help, of course. Now won't that be fun, Kingy?" Galdon turned and crept out of the room. He locked the door behind him and left Dlemar all alone in the darkness with his hands and feet tied to a chair.

Dlemar spat on the food beside him, for he knew that it probably contained some kind of evil potion that would somehow help this insane mage put the Crown on his head. He would rather die of starvation than be used in this evil man's plans. He had to escape.

All of his hopes disappeared, however, when he heard the

sounds of guards outside his door. He looked to the only source of light he had, a small barred window on the other side of the room. He stared into the moonlight, and for miles all he could see were hundreds of snow-capped mountains. He was trapped.

Both NeShae and Alex were up and out of their separate rooms before dawn, and they both made their way to the table, where Artimus had kindly prepared breakfast. "Good morning," he said to them as they sat down and began to eat. They also gave their greetings as they thought of what was ahead of them. They were both anxious to begin their journey into peril. They finished the meal quickly and looked to Artimus in an excited but worried fashion.

"We should be on our way," Alex said as he stood up and placed his sword in the scabbard at his side. It hung gracefully from the suit of full chain-mail armor he was wearing.

"Yes, we should," NeShae agreed as she too stood up, dressed in her normal apparel, trousers and a work shirt, with a short sword hanging at her waist.

"Before you go," Artimus said suddenly, "I have some things for you that should aid you in your quest."

He reached into a large chest and pulled out a long bow. It was silver in color, with strange golden engravings carved perfectly about it. It was truly the most beautiful bow that either Alex or NeShae had ever seen.

Artimus handed the bow to Alex and said, "This weapon will help you greatly. It needs no arrows, and will pierce the armor of many a foe."

Alex took the bow with a look of awe and said, "I thank you, great elf. I am forever in your debt. But may I ask, if it needs no arrows, how does it fire?"

Artimus grinned and said, "Why don't you pull it back and see?"

Alex held the perfectly crafted bow up and drew the string back. It almost seemed to pull itself, it was so light and easy to draw. As soon as the string was drawn fully, a shimmer of light appeared in place of an arrow. It was nearly invisible to all except Alex, who saw it as clearly as he could see his own hand. He took a few steps toward the open door, and carefully took aim at an old fallen tree outside. He released the magical arrow and watched as it soared through the air at an incredible rate and struck the tree exactly where Alex had aimed. It tore completely through it and into the next one. Alex could only stare at the weapon in awe. What power this item contained!

NeShae stared at the two, amazed, as she wondered if she, too, would get a gift such as this.

Artimus again reached into the chest and this time pulled out a beautifully carved oak staff. He handed it to NeShae and said, "This weapon handles well, and will fell enemies with a single strike. It also has many other powers that you will learn about in the future."

One more time Artimus reached into the chest, and this time he pulled out two small vials, each containing a deep blue liquid. "These are potions of healing," he continued. "There is enough for two doses in each vial, so use them carefully and only when you absolutely have to."

They thanked Artimus one last time for all of his help, exchanged hugs and farewells, and continued out to where their horses and gear awaited them. They mounted their horses and looked to Artimus one more time. "Farewell for now, my friends," Artimus sang out as he raised a hand to wave good-bye, "for we will meet again."

Together, NeShae and Alex rode off to find the road that would lead them to Donaville and Merquill the Sage.

Galdon quietly crept into the room of his captive. After several hours, he had finally fallen asleep. Now it was time to put the Crown on his head. Galdon raised the sacred artifact he had brought into the room and made his way over to Dlemar's slouching figure. Galdon excitedly lowered the Crown into position. But just as it was about ready to rest perfectly on Dlemar's head, the king's eyes opened and he threw his head back, knocking the Crown from Galdon's hands and sending it crashing to the floor.

"Fool! You can't destroy the Crown," Galdon screamed at the king just inches from his face. "It looks as though I'll have to weaken you a bit before our conquest can begin. How long can you go without food, my dear King?"

Galdon was so close to Dlemar's face that the king could smell his rancid breath. It made him sick, and Galdon knew it. Then a feeling of anger came over Dlemar because of the helpless position he was in, and he spat in his face. In the same breath he yelled at the mage, "I would die before I would let you have the pleasure of seeing me grovel at your feet."

Galdon stood up slowly and wiped his face with his sleeve. He showed little emotion, but Dlemar knew he was angry. He got proof when he felt a sharp backhand strike his face. Dlemar could feel a small trickle of blood run down his cheek, and then looked to the doorway where Galdon was about to exit. He saw the hatred in the mage's eyes as he heard him say in a vengeful voice, "You will pay, King."

Alex and NeShae continued down the road leading to Donaville for the entire day. They traveled as fast as they thought the horses could handle. The road on which they were riding connected in Terrigrin with the two trade routes: the Route of Gold, and the Giver's Trail. Because of this, there were also many caravans on this path to Donaville. But before Donaville was another, named Baulden, which was one of Donaville's rivals when it came to sea cargo and trading, for both of these cities were only about three days of land travel between them.

"How long did Artimus say it would take to reach Baulden?" NeShae questioned as they rode.

"He said five to seven days, depending on the weather," Alex answered.

"Then we will make it in four," NeShae said loudly, trying to overcome the sound of the horses' hooves.

Alex pulled back on his horse and slowed to a trot. Seeing this, NeShae did the same.

Then he spoke, "Are you crazy? That would mean we'd have to ride on through the night also."

NeShae's smile showed that that was what she was, in fact, thinking.

"But the horses—" Alex continued, "they need a rest."

"We can stop at the next stream to eat and rest the horses. Then we can continue."

Alex knew he couldn't argue with his determined companion, so with a sigh he agreed and they continued on their way.

A few hours later, as dusk was approaching, they finally came to a small creek that ran smoothly across the road. There was a small grassy area off to one side where they decided to set up a camp to rest. They quickly dismounted as Alex told NeShae, "I'll go find what little firewood there is around here if you will tend to the horses." NeShae agreed and they went their separate ways to complete their tasks.

A little while later, Alex came back with a load of firewood in his arms. He looked at the camp they had made and saw the horses resting contentedly as they drank from the trickling stream. NeShae was busy preparing the food that would be their supper that night.

Alex arranged the firewood in the middle of the camp and went to his backpack to get flint to light the fire. NeShae saw this and walked calmly over to the firepit and grabbed one of the logs. She sat there for a few moments and concentrated, as Alex looked on. From her fingers came a dull red glow that extended onto the log, and still she concentrated. Soon the entire log was burning. Alex watched, amazed.

"Where...how did you..." he stuttered.

"It's another one of my abilities that I was born with," she answered without giving it another thought.

"You never cease to amaze me," the prince said seriously, as he and NeShae began eating.

"I am now worthy to hold your amazement?" NeShae said jokingly. "What brought on this sudden change?"

The prince looked at the ground and thought for a moment.

"Artimus," he said. Then he slowly raised his head and looked into those beautiful green eyes of NeShae's and spoke, "And you."

As they gazed into each other's eyes, their problems seemed to be removed, as though nothing else mattered at that moment. After a few minutes they both finished their meager supper and NeShae finally said, "We better get packed and continue on."

Alex reluctantly agreed, so they continued on their journey into the moonlit night. They rode nonstop the entire night, and only rested for a few hours the next morning for breakfast. Again they rode on during the warm sunny day. They had been lucky, for the weather was on their side.

Toward evening, they saw in the distance a small wagon, so they gradually slowed their pace. "Most likely merchants or a trade wagon," NeShae said calmly.

"Most likely, but not for certain," Alex responded suspiciously. His training with Artimus was in the back of his mind, and he knew to expect anything.

They stayed on their course, which led them straight up to the wagon, where they saw three men standing outside smoking long curled pipes. They acknowledged the two riders, but they paid little attention to them until Alex spoke, "Excuse me, gentlemen, but do you know how far we are from Baulden?"

"About two days' travel," the stockiest one of the three said. Evidently he was their leader. "Why? Who are you?"

"I am Prince Alexander Denmoore of the Terrigrin Castle, and this is..." The prince hesitated, not knowing how he should introduce NeShae.

"I am his wife, NeShae Denmoore, and we are very hungry, for we have traveled far. Would you mind if we camped with you on this fine night?" NeShae finished for Alex, as she gave him a quick wink. Alex smiled at NeShae's words. His wife? The more he thought about it, the better it sounded.

"Of course not," the leader said happily as he tossed a look to one of the other men. "We have an open tent waiting, and fresh food on the fire. It would be our pleasure to have you stay with us this evening."

The three men, who were all dressed in very elaborate clothes, seemed very generous, Alex thought to himself. In fact, maybe too generous. He dismissed the thought and made his way to where he could rest his horse. NeShae followed quickly behind, preferring to stay with her "husband" instead of the three men who were eyeing her so suggestively.

They were both very tired at this point and ate little before they went to their designated tent to get some much-needed sleep. As soon as they left the company of the other men, they heard whispers coming from their hosts' direction. NeShae shrugged them off, but Alex couldn't. The prince knew that he would get little sleep that night.

They entered the tent and found that it was a very cozy little shelter. There was a burning lantern in the middle sitting next to the one large cloth bed. NeShae and Alex looked at each other, neither of them knowing what to do. Then they heard a voice outside ask if everything were okay.

"Just fine," Alex said, not changing his unsure look at NeShae. "Thanks."

"I can sleep over here next to the wall. You can take the bed," Alex spoke as soon as he heard the footsteps of the stranger disappear.

"But won't you get cold?" NeShae asked, concerned.

"I'll be fine. You just get some rest," Alex assured her.

"All right, if you insist," NeShae agreed as she started removing some of her clothes. Alex could hardly stay standing long enough to turn his back away from NeShae to allow her the privacy that she hadn't ask for. Alex tried to focus on the events that lay in front of him, but he found it hard when one of the most beautiful girls he had ever seen was undressing behind him. He looked down to find himself biting his fist as he told NeShae in a squeaky voice, "Good night, my lady."

With a teasing chuckle, NeShae answered, "Good night, my husband." Then she turned the lantern out and went to sleep.

Alex did not sleep, however, for he thought of the three men outside who had so graciously taken NeShae and him in. He wondered if they would have been so generous if he weren't a prince.

"Patrick, now's the time. They should be asleep by now," one of the men whispered. Without another word, the dark-haired man crept silently to the tent where the two unsuspecting victims slept. Or so he thought.

Alex barely heard the sound of the tent flap opening as he opened his eyes and tried to clear the sleepiness away. He was careful not to make any sudden move as he watched the intruder enter the tent. He studied him as the man quietly picked up the prince's moneybag, which Alex had so conveniently placed there. The thief gracefully made his way around the tent until he came up next to Alex. What a beautiful bow, the burglar thought to himself. He had to have it.

As he brought his gaze again to the bow, he noticed something else. The prince's eyes were open and staring at him!

"Looking for something?" Alex asked calmly as the frightened thief started to back out of the tent.

He only made it a few steps before Alex with lightening quick speed, slit his throat. Alex took his possessions back from the thief and woke NeShae up quietly. He told her the story and asked her to stay in the tent while he took care of some business.

"Be careful," NeShae pleaded as Alex silently left the tent and made his way over to the campfire where the two other men were standing and waiting. All of their gear was packed, and they were ready to leave as soon as Patrick came out with the loot.

They saw a dark figure emerge from the tent. Thinking it was their other companion, they quietly approached him, just in time to realize that they were standing face to face with the prince, the man they had tried to steal from. the prince had no tolerance for thieves of this sort, and there was no look of mercy in his eyes as he cut the head cleanly from his second victim of the evening. The only one left was the leader, who was almost trembling in fear.

"Get your sword," Alex said in a deep commanding voice.

"Wh…what?" the confused man stuttered.

"Get your sword!" Alex screamed into the night. "You will die, but not without a weapon in your hands."

The man almost dropped to his knees to beg for his life, but he knew it would do no good, so he went to the other side of the wagon to get his sword. Alex stood patiently and waited until he realized that the man wasn't coming back. He turned just in time to see the man riding his horse across the open area away from the encampment.

"Good-bye, Prince!" he shouted and laughed into the moonlight.

Alex said nothing, but drew his bow. The string felt cool to his touch as he easily pulled it back and watched a magical arrow appear. He let go, and watched as the bolt of light ripped right through the rider's body and sailed into the night. The man fell to the ground, dead, as his horse continued into the darkness.

"Good-bye, thief," was Alex's only reply.

"Not bad for a spoiled child," NeShae's voice sounded as Alex spun around to meet her gaze. She held out a small wooden container for Alex to look at. "I found it in the wagon when you were finishing your business. I wonder what's in it?"

Alex took the chest to examine it. He pulled out one of his daggers and pried the poorly made lock off. Then they looked inside.

"ABSENCE MAKES THE HEART"

As Alex pulled the contents from the chest, NeShae looked on, excited to see what they could be. As she got a full view, her face turned to a confused look as she asked, "Why would anyone keep an old patched cloak in a locked chest?"

Alex looked just as confused at his finding and shrugged his shoulders. "I have no idea," he said, bewildered. "Maybe there's something in the pockets."

They checked both of the brown cloak's pockets but found nothing, so they decided to carefully examine the rest of the item. As NeShae looked closely at the odd-colored patches which were placed quite frequently about the cloak, she noticed that all of them were miniature pictures of different items. One, for instance, was an exact replica of a lantern, another was a rope, and yet another of the many patches was in the shape of a small cart. The puzzled look on NeShae's face perfectly matched the one on Alex's.

"Why would anyone go to all the trouble of making such beautiful patches for such an old piece of clothing?" Alex asked, not really expecting any answer.

"I don't know," she said, feeling on one of the patches a small gem which had caught her eye. "Perhaps it's a magical cloak. Should I try it on?"

Alex looked at her indecisively, trying to decide which answer would be best, so NeShae grabbed the robe from him and put it on over her clothes.

"It feels warm," NeShae explained as they stood in the cool breeze of the night. "It's as though it can sense the chill of the air and is giving me warmth."

Then she reached down to one of the patches and gently tugged on its outline. In the blink of an eye, an iron battle ax appeared in her hand, an exact duplicate of the patch she had just pulled on.

Alex's surprise caused him to jump back a few steps as he watched this mystical event in disbelief. "It is magical!" he shouted excitedly. "See if you can put the ax back."

Alex watched as NeShae replaced the battle ax just as easily as she had taken it from the cloak. They tested the magical piece of clothing further, trying to discover its limitations, and learned that only three items at a time could be removed. They even found that when they replaced the lantern patch, it became filled with oil for the next time it was needed. Alex noticed another change in the cloak that NeShae didn't. As soon as she had donned the item, the patches disappeared, and its appearance turned into that of a new brown velvet cloak. To NeShae the cloak looked the same, and she could easily see all of the items. She closely examined every patch and named them for Alex, just in case they should need them in the future. "Two daggers, a lantern, one rope, a cart, a battle ax, a bag of something…I think it's coins, a gem, one ladder, and a small raft."

"This could prove very helpful," Alex said with a hopeful

smile. "But for now, we should get some sleep; we have a long road ahead."

"I agree," NeShae said as she removed the cloak and made her way to the tent, followed by Alex.

"Now that there are a few tents left unoccupied, I suppose I can sleep in one of those," Alex said politely.

"Nonsense," NeShae argued. "It would take an hour or so to set one up anyway. Besides, there's plenty of room for two in this one."

Alex's heart almost jumped from his chest as he heard NeShae utter those words. He tried not to show his initial excitement, though, and said calmly, "Well, if you insist." He couldn't help showing her a small smile.

Alex made his way over to the far side of the tent, where he had been before. Just then, he heard NeShae ask in a quiet voice, "Are you scared of me?"

"Of course not," Alex answered after a short chuckle.

"Then why is it you choose to sleep on the other side of the tent instead of near me?" NeShae asked in a shaky, troubled voice.

"Well, I didn't mean to...if you would have told me...I don't know," Alex answered, knowing that he would gladly sleep near her if she were only to ask.

NeShae didn't say another word as she rolled over under her blanket and closed her eyes. As she tried to fall asleep, she thought to herself, how much more of an invitation does he need? Or maybe he understood, but just didn't want to be near her. NeShae tried to hold back the tears that were forming in her eyes, but she couldn't, so she quietly cried herself to sleep.

Alex wanted badly to stand up and go over to NeShae, but he couldn't bring himself to do it. She had called him so many names in the last month that he couldn't bring himself to believe she had feelings for him. "If only I knew," Alex said softly as he, too, closed his eyes and drifted into sleep.

Dlemar's hands and feet ached from the ropes he had been wearing for the last two days. This was the first day he had not been sent any food. But, in truth, he had not eaten for two days, ever since he had been captured. the king wondered how his wife was doing and if she were okay. Then his thoughts turned to his son, Alex, and Artimus, his age-old friend. "Artimus," he whispered to himself, "I need your help once again, my dear friend."

Dlemar dropped his head and let his exhausted body get the rest that it was longing for.

Alex awoke the next morning and stretched as he slowly opened his eyes. After a few moments, he looked over to NeShae, only to find that she was gone. He rushed over to the jumble of blankets, but he saw that she was nowhere in sight. He grabbed his sword and dashed out of the tent, just in time to see NeShae packing her gear.

"Good morning," Alex spoke, relieved to find her outside.

"Why did you rush from the tent? More burglars?" NeShae said dryly, as she continued tying packs to the horses.

"I woke up and saw that you were gone. I thought something had happened."

"And you'd care if something did happen?" she said in an obvious voice of anger.

This confused the prince and he stated, "Of course I'd care. Why wouldn't I?"

NeShae stopped what she was doing, turned to him, and screamed, "Just because I'm not a princess or of royalty doesn't mean I'm stupid!" She paused as she tried to stop the tears that were rolling down her face. "I know when I'm not wanted. I'll continue the search on my own, which will free you from my peasant stupidity."

Alex was shocked at her angry choice of words, and could only manage to get out the words, "Would you just tell me what I've done?"

"Done?" NeShae asked with tears still falling. She then whipped around and again began packing what little gear was left. She said, just loud enough for Alex to hear, "It's more what you haven't done."

Alex couldn't hold back anymore. He had to say what he was thinking. "First of all, quit your crying. Second, this isn't just my fault, so don't blame it all on me." He walked over to her, gently took her arm, and turned her toward him. He carefully wiped the remaining tears from her eyes and spoke in a caring, calm voice, "NeShae, if you think for one moment that I do not care, then you are wrong, indeed. I care much more than you think, and I would have told you that, but I didn't know how you'd react."

NeShae stopped her crying and looked deeply into Alex's eyes. "But what about last night? I couldn't have told you how I felt in a more straightforward way."

"I know," Alex sighed. "I guess I'm just too dumb to take a hint." They both laughed and Alex continued, "And please don't ever throw another one of these temper tantrums, okay?"

"Okay," NeShae answered slowly as Alex leaned toward her. Then he heard footsteps behind him. He turned quickly and saw two green, deformed, and ugly creatures running in their direction with swords in their hands. They stood only about three feet tall but looked as though they were familiar with battle. Alex recognized them as goblins. The prince drew his sword, positioning himself in front of NeShae as her protection. Both of the goblins arrived at the same time and found that Alex was more than ready for them. With one quick strike of his sword, one of the goblin's arms was lying on the ground. As Alex parried a blow from the other monster, he pulled one of his daggers from his belt and threw it into the air. It struck the second goblin in the throat, and the prince watched as the creature toppled to the ground. The one-armed goblin saw this and started running as fast as his legs could carry him away from the master swordsman. Alex started to follow, but NeShae grabbed his arm and pleaded, "There's been enough killing. Let the poor creature go."

Alex started to protest, but finally agreed and said, "Okay, but if we ever see a one-armed goblin near here again, he won't be so lucky."

At those words they both broke out into laughter. Then

Alex pulled NeShae close to him and gave her a long warm hug. Both of them felt much better since their last conversation, and they decided to continue on their way. They mounted their horses and once again rode toward Baulden. Later that evening they came to a small wooded area in the mostly barren land.

"Should we camp here for the night?" NeShae asked as they drew near.

"We might as well. It should serve as some protection from the dangers of the night," Alex answered her.

They stopped and dismounted, eager to rest their weary backs and legs from the long day's ride. They fixed some dried meat, which Artimus had given them, and then sat next to each other by the warm glowing campfire.

"We should try to get some sleep," NeShae said with a gleam in her eyes.

"You should try to, yes," Alex told her. "But I'll stay up and keep watch. There's no telling what kinds of creatures wander around here at night."

NeShae, sounding disappointed, said, "All right, but promise me you'll wake me up when it's my turn to keep watch. Okay?"

"Okay," the prince said as he smiled and walked over to a fallen tree that would serve as his night-watch position.

NeShae pulled her few blankets around her as she lay next to the brightly burning fire. Then she thought about what had just happened and mumbled to herself, "I know he hates me; I know it. Why else would he leave me for an old tree? I'm making a fool of myself; I know I am." She paused for a moment, then started again, "I just wish he would kiss me!"

She couldn't take it anymore. She threw the blankets back, stood up, and walked over to where the prince was sitting, watching the darkness. NeShae marched over to Alex, grabbed his head, and gave him a long passionate kiss. The prince didn't seem to protest, however, and when she was finished, she didn't say a word but walked back to the campfire and lay down to go to sleep.

Alex sat stunned, with his mouth still open, on the log,

wondering what had just happened. He shook his head to make sure he was still awake, and then looked to NeShae. There she was, underneath some blankets, her eyes closed, with a large grin on her face.

The next morning came quickly for NeShae as she felt Alex gently touch her shoulder. "Is it time for my watch already?" she asked.

"No," he answered, "it's time to pack up and get to Baulden."

NeShae opened her eyes and noticed the truth of his words, for the sun was already starting to make its appearance on the horizon. "But why didn't you wake me for a watch?"

"Because you are so beautiful when you sleep," Alex complimented her.

"And I'm not when I'm awake?" she asked sarcastically as the prince blushed. They both laughed at the incident, then fixed some breakfast before they packed their gear and once again continued their journey.

Galdon entered the chamber and saw King Dlemar, who was still tied to the chair in the middle of the barren room. Dlemar gave the mage a threatening stare and growled, "As soon as I am free, I'm going to rip your heart out with my bare hands."

"Such words, Kingy," Galdon said mockingly. "But how do you plan on getting free? Do you think your aged elf friend will help rescue you? He is so old. Perhaps the king's Guard? It's too bad they are all dead. I've got it," he said as he snapped his fingers, "Your son, the prince, will save you! He is so obedient and trustworthy, wouldn't you say, Kingy?"

Dlemar shouted in anger as he made a lunge for the wizard, but then remembered that he was tied to the chair. His momentum was stopped abruptly as Galdon looked at him and sneered, "No one can help you, and you can only go for so long without food. Face it, Kingy, soon we will rule the city of Terrigrin together!" His voice rang throughout his tower as the mage evilly petted the golden Crown he held in his hands.

NeShae and Alex could see the town of Baulden in the distance, and it filled their hearts with excitement, for they had traveled the entire day and were anxious to find Merquill the Sage. They reached the large harbor city near dusk and continued in to find a place to rest the horses and get information on Merquill. They left their mounts to be cared for in the stables and started down the street to find an inn. The One Stop Inn was right across the street, so they decided to see if they could find a place to sleep for the night. They agreed to first check out the bar area, in hopes of finding someone who knew where Merquill lived.

As they entered the first room of the inn, they found that it was a very busy place, with all different kinds of people drinking and spilling ale around the noise-filled room. In a few rare spots they saw sailors lying on their faces after one too many drinks. Evidently it had been a long time since some of them had seen land.

Alex and NeShae shoved their way through the commotion to the bar and ordered two mugs of ale. Alex paid the man and they sat down to watch the others around them. Right next to them sat an old, hunched-over man with a long gray beard and a deep scar across his left cheek. Alex couldn't help but stare at the wound on the man's face and felt a little embarrassed when the stranger turned to face him and NeShae.

"It's from a shark who didn't like the looks of my body in is water," the man said, answering Alex's unasked question.

"I'm sorry; I didn't mean to stare," the prince replied politely.

"No need to apologize, son. It's not the first time. I'm Hans, one of the very first sailors around these parts. And who might this pretty young lady ye've got here be?" the man asked.

"This is…my wife, NeShae," Alex answered as he gave her a warm smile, "and I am Alex." He didn't know if he should reveal that he was a prince or not, so he decided to wait.

"What brings ye to Baulden?" Hans asked them.

"We're looking for a man named Merquill, a sage who supposedly lives near Donaville. Do you know of him?" Alex asked, hoping the man could help them.

"Sorry, never heard of the guy," Hans answered. Just as the old sailor was going to ask them another question, they heard a man scream something in a horrible voice which was heard clearly over the rest of the noise in the room. All three of them turned to see a huge muscular man yelling at a small, skinny, black-haired boy. The man pushed the boy back and watched as he crashed to the floor.

"Thought ye could get away with picking me pocket, eh, boy?" the enormous man said in a harsh tone. The rest of the crowded inn seemed to stop as all eyes were focused on the two.

Alex started to get up, but felt Hans's arm pull him back. Alex looked at him questioningly as Hans whispered, "That's Careet, the strongest man in Baulden. He can crush an orc's skull with one blow. He ain't one to be a-messin' with, son. Ya hear me?"

NeShae, too, grabbed Alex and pleaded, "He's much bigger than you, Alex. Please don't do anything."

Alex's eyes took on a cold angry stare as he watched the man kick the child again and again in the stomach. Then he turned to NeShae's beautiful face and said, "But quickness will beat strength nine out of ten times." He gave her a small smile as he remembered Artimus telling him this when they first met.

Hans had heard their conversation and told Alex in a concerned tone, "Well, let's hope you aren't the unlucky one, then."

Alex stood up, and to the amazement of every other person in the inn, strolled right over to the man who was cruelly teasing the helpless boy. Alex positioned himself directly behind the giant of a man and tried to draw as much courage as he could before he said out loud, "Hey, orc breath, why don't you push me around instead of that helpless kid?"

The man turned around, outraged that someone had defied him, and charged Alex. The prince had expected this, and stood still until the very last second, when he ducked and rolled out of the man's reach. The clumsy giant continued on and crashed into a table full of people and landed on the floor. Alex's angry opponent quickly got to his feet and this time threw a wild punch. Alex easily dodged it and gave the large man three quick jabs in the nose and mouth before he even knew what hit him. This stunned him, and the man stumbled back a few feet as he felt the blood trickle down his face.

Then Alex jeered, "A little different when they hit back, huh?" The entire inn was now in total silence as everyone watched this newcomer's strength and agility.

Alex's last comment really made the man mad, for he took a huge roundhouse swing at the prince with all the strength he could find. The punch just grazed Alex as he ducked out of reach, and the prince saw his chance. The momentum of the giant's punch carried him almost completely around, into a perfect position for Alex to land punch after punch into his face and midsection. Within seconds, the giant bully lay in a crumpled form on the floor, with blood streaming from at least three different places on his body. Alex could have easily finished him off, but he looked to NeShae and saw her shaking her head no, as if he should let the man be. So he did.

The Inn was still silent as the prince walked slowly back to NeShae and Hans. Alex looked around and saw that everyone was staring at him in disbelief. Then he yelled to the whole inn, "What? What are you starin' at?" It didn't take long for the regular noise of the inn to pop back into motion. Alex looked to NeShae again as she wiped the small amount of blood from his face that was the result of the giant's grazing punch. Her only remark was, "Must you be so valiant?"

By this time, the small boy who had been the large man's target of abuse had painfully made his way over to where Alex was standing. The boy looked no older than about sixteen and was dirty and grungy looking. He was bent over somewhat from the beating he had taken earlier. His tired eyes looked at

Alex as he said, "Thank you, sir. No one's ever stuck up for me before. Who knows what would have happened if you wouldn't have been here. How can I repay you?"

Alex laughed and said jokingly, "Take me to Merquill the Sage," as though he expected the boy to tell him he had never heard of the man.

But instead, the boy answered, "Okay, when do we leave?"

Both NeShae and Alex looked at him in surprise. "You know where this sage lives?" Alex asked, trying to hide his excitement.

"Well, I'm not sure of the name, but I know of only one sage around here. The one I know of lives near Donaville," the boy said.

"That's the one we're looking for. What's your name, kid?" the prince asked.

"Everyone calls me R.C.," he answered.

"R.C.?" NeShae asked. "But why?"

"It stands for Rat Child," the boy said slowly with his head down, ashamed of his given name.

"But why would anyone…" Alex started.

"Because I have no home and steal for a living. I live with the rats," he explained.

"But what of your parents?" NeShae asked in a caring, motherly tone.

"They were killed by some soldiers when I was six. They refused to pay the higher taxes that the king had set. So I've been living on the streets ever since," R.C. told them.

"Well, first of all, we have to get you a different name," NeShae said comfortingly. "How about…Matthew?"

The boy's eyes lit up as he heard the sound of his newfound name. "It sounds wonderful," he said with a smile as he repeated the name over and over again.

"Well, Matthew, why don't you come with us?" Alex asked.

"Where to?" Matthew asked suspiciously.

"To get something to eat," Alex answered.

"How do I know I can trust you?" the boy replied.

Alex looked at him and grinned. "You, a person who makes his living by theft, is asking if you can trust me? Shouldn't it be the other way around?"

They all chuckled for a moment, and said nothing more. They waved good-bye to Hans, who was now mingling with some barmaids, and then walked into the next room of the inn. It was smaller than the first and had a large wooden desk placed directly across from the entrance. Behind it sat a young man, perhaps in his late teens, who asked, "May I help you folks?"

"Yes," Alex replied. "We're looking for a place to sleep and some nice hot food."

"How many rooms would you like, sir?"

Alex looked at NeShae, who was blushing a little at the question, but still managed to give the prince a warm smile. Without removing his stare from hers, Alex said, "Two." NeShae's warm look turned into that of a helpless and sad- dened child, until Alex again spoke, "One for this boy."

The man at the desk took the two pieces of gold Alex handed him and gave them the keys to their adjacent rooms. "Supper will be brought to you in a few minutes," he told them.

Matthew was extremely pleased at being invited to sleep in a real bed, and found himself liking the two strangers more and more with each passing moment. They climbed the stairs to where their rooms awaited them, and at Alex's request, Matthew joined them for supper. As soon as the meals arrived, all three ate ravenously, but none quite as fast as Matthew. His huge pile of food was gone before Alex or NeShae were even halfway done with theirs.

After they were finished, the three of them sat back to relax as Alex and NeShae told Matthew all about their journey so far. They told him about the magical cloak they had found, Ben's wound, Alex's father, the king, and where they were headed.

Matthew sat listening, eyes wide open the entire time, intrigued by each and every detail until he couldn't wait any longer and blurted out, "Well, certainly you must need another companion to aid you on your quest. Let me come with—I promise I won't disappoint you," he pleaded as NeShae and Alex looked at each other, each searching for an answer.

"How about this," Alex offered as an answer. "We'll talk about it and let you know before we start our journey to Donaville tomorrow morning. Okay?"

"Okay," Matthew answered in a dull tone. "Just one last thing. Could I see your money bag for a moment?"

Alex answered his request with a confused look, but nonetheless agreed and reached for the money bag that was tied to his waist. It was gone! He looked to Matthew for the answer and watched as the young boy tossed Alex the bag that he had so easily taken.

"You could use me in your party," Matthew said with a grin as he stood up and walked to the door. "Thanks for letting me stay here tonight, and for saving my life." Then he left to find his room.

As soon as he was gone, NeShae cuddled up to Alex, put her arms around one of his biceps, and said softly, "We really could use another companion."

"I know, but he's so young. He has no idea what he's getting into," Alex said, more to himself than to NeShae.

"What kind of life does he have here?" NeShae asked Alex, trying to convince him to bring Matthew along. "He must steal to survive and constantly stares death in the face. If he were with us at least he could look at death with friends. Let's give him a chance, Alex. Please?"

Alex watched her beautiful lips as she spoke, looking for some flaw in her reasoning. But there was none. "You're right," he said after a moment of thought. "Now let's get some sleep."

NeShae's face molded into a look of hurt. "What? You want to get some sleep? Now?" she questioned him in a loud angry voice.

"Yes," the prince answered in a quiet voice, "We have to remember why we're here, and what we have in front of us." Alex grabbed one of the extra blankets and covered himself as he stretched out on the floor. NeShae saw this and flung herself back into the large pillow that was awaiting her head.

"Of course. Remember why we're here," was all she said before Alex turned the lantern off, and they both drifted into sleep.

They awoke the next morning and found Matthew waiting patiently outside the door. "Good morning," NeShae growled, as she barely looked at Matthew but continued down the hallway toward the eating area. His eyebrows rose questioningly as he asked Alex sarcastically, "What puts her in such a chipper mood this morning?"

"I'm not sure. I think her pillow was too hard." Matthew looked at him with a strange smile but pushed the subject no further. They simply followed NeShae down to where breakfast was being served.

After a few moments at the table, NeShae's mood began to improve, much to the delight of both Alex and Matthew. Every once in a while she would give the prince a warm smile, which puzzled Alex, but also gave him even more respect for this unique woman than he had felt before. While Matthew was getting another plate of fresh eggs, NeShae looked at him with love-filled eyes and said, "You were right; I'm sorry. I shouldn't have put my feeling before our purpose. Do you forgive me?"

"How could I not?" the prince said as he gently lifted her hand to his lips and kissed it.

When they were finished eating, Matthew looked to them with hopeful eyes and asked, "Did you decide if I could come with you yet?"

Before Alex could speak, NeShae answered his question. "Yes, we have, and we'd be honored if you would join us— on one condition:" she continued as the boy's face lit up excitedly, "that you listen to us and do exactly as we say at all times. Agreed?"

"Definitely," Matthew said, almost too overcome with joy to speak. "Well, let's get going. Time's wastin' and we aren't getting any closer to your father or that weapon." They couldn't have said it better themselves.

From there they crossed the street to where the stables and their horses were. Inside, Alex told Matthew to pick out a horse, so he carefully studied each and every one of the available horses. Finally, his eyes came to rest on a medium-sized, entirely black mare. "That one," he said as he pointed to the majestic horse.

Alex paid the man for the new mount and then went to find their other horses. Matthew thanked Alex again and again as he clumsily tried to let his new mount know who was boss. His unfamiliarity with the animal was obvious, however, and Alex and NeShae watched and chuckled at the boy and his horse as the three of them rode out of Baulden.

"How far is it to Merquill's?" NeShae asked Matthew as soon as they had left the city.

"That depends on whether we take the well-traveled road or the not-so-safe wilderness. The road takes six days; the wilderness five," he answered.

"Then we take the wilderness," Alex said with an agreeing look from NeShae.

"As you say," Matthew said as he veered slowly off the well-built road and into the wide barren fields. There were patches of small forests scattered here and there, but the majority of the land was plain. The three companions traveled quite a distance the first day, and finally came to rest on the edge of a small cluster of trees just as the sun was setting. As they were setting up camp that evening, Alex asked Matthew how he knew where Merquill lived.

"Well, I've never actually been there before," he explained, "but I know right where it is. When you live on the street for ten years, you learn things. All kinds of things," he said with a smile.

"Do you know what this Merquill is like?" Alex asked, trying to learn more about the man he was hopefully going to meet.

"All I know is that people come from hundreds of miles

around to learn from him. But very few people know what he looks like. He lives so far away from everything," Matthew answered. Off in the distance, they heard a great clap of thunder as they watched the sky grow darker by the minute.

"We better set the tent up before it starts storming," NeShae said as she made supper over their small campfire. Alex and Matthew grabbed the large tent that they had taken from the three thieves just a few nights earlier. As soon as they had finished setting it up, the three of them sat down to eat NeShae's meal.

When they were finished, Alex stood up and said with a yawn, "You two should get some sleep. I'll keep watch just in case anything wanders too close to our camp."

NeShae jumped up and ordered firmly, "Absolutely not! You always keep watch and never get any sleep. Matthew and I can take turns keeping watch while you get some much-needed sleep."

Alex looked into her stern eyes and started, "But—"

"That's what we're doing, so don't even argue," NeShae said with finality in her voice. "Matthew and I will keep watch while you get some sleep."

"What if something happens?" Alex asked her.

"Then believe me, you'll be the first to know about it. Okay?" NeShae compromised, hoping that Alex would agree.

"Okay," he answered softly, "but only if you promise to wake me for even the smallest of noises."

"I promise," she said as she kissed him on the cheek. "Matthew, why don't you take the first shift while Alex and I try to get a little sleep," she continued.

"Sure," he answered, trying to hide the grin that was forming on his face.

Another clap of thunder shook the ground as more and more streaks of lightning brightened the evening sky. A light rain began to fall as Alex and NeShae entered their tent together and left Matthew alone in the dark storm to keep watch over them. A few hours later, with the rain still falling, NeShae appeared from the tent and quietly walked over to where Matthew was sitting, sword in hand, watching the blackness.

"Anything happen while I was gone?" NeShae asked him as she sat down next to him.

"Nope. Not yet, anyway," Matthew answered, not removing his eyes from the darkness around them.

"You should get some sleep; we have a long day ahead of us tomorrow," NeShae continued.

"I suppose," he said slowly, although he made no move to leave. There was silence for a few minutes until Matthew finally said, "He loves you a lot, you know."

"Who? Alex?" NeShae asked with a smile on her face as the rain continued to dampen her clothes. "How can you be so sure?"

"I can see it easily when he looks at you. The way he listens to you. He can shame Baulden's strongest man, but is humbled by you. Even if he does not say it, he loves you," Matthew told her.

"Well, I wish I was as sure as you. He acts as though he has feelings for me, but whenever we are together he turns me away. Maybe he still only thinks of me as his peasant servant," NeShae said as she thought about the last few days with the prince.

"He has a lot on his mind, just like you. Maybe he's just thinking about his dad. Look, trust me on this one. The guy cares for you, okay?" Matthew stated flatly with no room for argument.

"I hope you're right," was all NeShae said as she, too, looked into the darkness and smiled.

Galdon stared deeply into his blackened orb, trying to understand what he was seeing. All of a sudden, his eyes lit up as he slammed his fist onto the table. "Curse that old coot Artimus! How dare he think that he can send three children out to defeat me!" He looked back to the crystal ball and saw two people, a young woman and a boy. He knew one more slept in the tent, but he couldn't tell who. Then he concentrated on another place as the image of the three companions faded, and another figure appeared.

"What do you want, Galdon?" the figure asked in a deep voice through the crystal ball.

"There are three humans on their way to Donaville at this moment. I want them stopped long before they get there," Galdon instructed.

"Where are they now?" the voice spoke again.

"One day's travel out of Baulden. Very close to you," Galdon answered.

"By tomorrow they will be of little worry to you," came the reply of the voice. "I will take care of it."

The image of the figure slowly faded as Galdon sat back and whispered, "I hope so."

Alex woke suddenly in a deep sweat and looked around. It was still dark out and the rain continued to pour. He guessed that sunrise was still two or three hours away. On the other side of the tent, Matthew was sleeping soundly. Then he remembered why he had awoken. Artimus! The vision returned clearly now; he had talked to Artimus in his sleep. He tried to think of what the elf said. Then it all came to him. The elf's exact words were, "Flee now; danger approaches."

"But it was just a dream," Alex reassured himself as he settled back down. "Unless he contacted me magically," he continued. Alex thought about it for a while and then stood up and started to dress, "It's better to be safe than dead. I trusted Artimus a few weeks ago, so why not now, even if it's in my dreams?" he told himself as he shook his head and slightly chuckled to himself. He woke Matthew and told him to get dressed, then went to find NeShae.

"I thought I told you to stay..." she started as soon as Alex appeared from the tent.

"Not now," he said sternly as he started to pack their gear. "We're leaving now; danger is near."

"Danger? But how..." she began to ask.

"Just pack!" he shouted over the noise of the storm. From

the look on his face, NeShae and Matthew (who had just exited the tent to join them) both knew that he was serious, so they didn't argue. In haste, the three of them threw all of their belongings onto their horses and started off into the black, stormy night.

They rode for two or three hours in the rain and darkness. Even though the sun had risen, the black clouds of the storm didn't allow it to shine.

Then NeShae yelled something as she pulled her mount to a stop. "Wait, I just remembered something." Alex and Matthew both looked at her questioningly. NeShae's face turned into a look of horror and desperation. "I forgot my staff at the camp!" she said as she started to cry. "I leaned it up against a tree when I was keeping watch." All of them knew that this was not good news if Alex had been right about danger approaching.

"I will go back," Alex said without any hint of emotion.

"No," NeShae sobbed, knowing that the danger could easily be behind them. "If you go, all of us go."

"Use some sense," Alex scolded her. "If something happens to all three of us, it's finished. But if something happens, and you two make it to Merquill's, maybe he can help rescue my father and get the weapon we need. Besides, one person travels faster than three." NeShae continued to cry uncontrollably at his words, but he continued, "Matthew, do you know how to use a bow?"

"Yes," Matthew answered, "but why don't we all stay together?" The tone in Matthew's voice showed that he, too, was scared.

Alex took the bow from his shoulder and gave it to Matthew. NeShae still wept as the two exchanged words. "Now, I want you to ride as fast as you can until you get to Merquill's. Stop only for short rests, until the horses can go again. Don't sleep; you'll have plenty of time at Merquill's. I'll be a few hours behind you, after I get NeShae's staff. I'll meet you at Merquill's, okay?"

"But are you sure you know the way?" Matthew asked,

still very concerned at what might happen to Alex, or to NeShae and him.

"By what you've told me, I think I can find it," he answered.

"Let's just leave the staff," NeShae choked out over her tears. "I don't need it."

Alex got off his horse and walked over to her. "Artimus said you would discover more powers of the staff in the future. It will be important, and we do need it. Now you stay with Matthew, and I'll be back before you know it." He kissed NeShae on the forehead and whispered, "I'll be back before you know it."

NeShae's tears started again as she just barely managed to say, "Be careful, Alex."

Alex walked over to Matthew again and looked into the boy's young face. "I need you to get her to Merquill. This is your chance to prove yourself, and I want you to protect her with your life, got it?" the prince's words were strong, but Matthew knew how much he cared for her.

"I'll get her to Merquill's or I'll die trying," Matthew said, suddenly feeling important with his new responsibility. But deep down, he truly wished that Alex would be with them.

Then Alex mounted, gave them both a final look, and rode off into the cold wet morning.

"We can't let him go," NeShae pleaded, still crying.

"We have to. He can take care of himself. We have to worry about getting to Merquill's safely," Matthew said reassuringly. "Now let's go."

With one last look in the prince's direction, NeShae finally agreed, unwillingly, and they started off to Merquill's, leaving the prince behind.

The dark figure emerged from the underbrush and picked up the oak staff and sniffed it. The scent was almost too obvious. It was them, the three that Galdon wanted dead. The girl owned the staff, and they had just left. He would wait there for a few hours until they were in the middle of the plains, with nowhere to run. Then he would feast.

Alex rode as fast as his horse would carry him until he finally reached the area where they had camped just a short time ago. It was quiet. There seemed to be no wind, even though it had been gusting just minutes before. There was a terrifying calmness to the camp, as though everything around him were watching him, waiting for his next move. the prince shrugged off his fear and walked over to where NeShae had left the staff. It was gone.

Matthew and NeShae stopped only for a few short meals and to briefly rest their horses before they continued on, getting closer to their destination with each passing hour, but farther away from Alex.

"Do you think he's all right?" NeShae asked Matthew in a worried voice.

"Of course he is," Matthew answered, unsure himself. "You underestimate Alex. I feel sorry for anything that tries to stop him from returning to you."

"My brother Ben told me the same thing when he left," NeShae said, remembering her brother's words. "He told me he'd be back before I knew it."

"Alex will be back," Matthew said as he looked into her eyes. "And soon after, so will your brother."

"Lookings for thisss?" a cold evil voice hissed behind Alex. The prince spun around quickly, his sword ready to meet whoever stood there.

Before Alex was a tall figure wearing a black cloak with a hood pulled up around its head. The figure was holding a short sword in one hand and had grabbed a battle ax with the other, as soon as he had thrown NeShae's staff to the ground in front of Alex. The face underneath the cloak wasn't visible, but from the sound of the figure's gravely hissing voice, Alex decided he didn't want to see it anyway.

"Howss would youss like to diess, my friends?" the voice

slurred. "By swordss, or by axess?"

"I wish I could return your hospitality and ask the same," the prince replied, "but I cannot, for I have only one means of killing you—by sword—and it will have to do."

Alex had hoped to anger the creature in front of him with these words, but it didn't work. He knew that a strong opponent stood in front of him.

The figure quickly lunged his sword at Alex's chest, hoping to end the battle early, but the prince was ready and parried the blow with ease. He returned a strike, only to see it deflected by the battle ax that stood in its way. The two exchanged harmless, lightening-quick attacks for what seemed like hours before Alex could feel himself starting to tire. His foe saw this and stepped back for a second, just enough time to pull his hood back, revealing his face.

Alex's arm dropped as he gazed at the face of something that had once been human, but clearly was not anymore. The features of the creature made Alex's eyes bulge in horror as he stared at the rotting flesh hanging from the creature's deformed face. The bone was visible in many places and his eyes were sockets with nothing but small greenish lights for eyes. The evil creature smiled as Alex let down his guard, and made a fluid swing with his short sword. It struck Alex in the left arm, just below his armor. The sword cut through the flesh and made a large gaping wound that sunk to the bone. Alex ignored the pain as the blood poured out, for he knew that if he hesitated again, it would mean his death.

Alex soon began to feel dizzy from the loss of blood, and he knew it would only be a matter of time before he fell unconscious. The deformed creature continued his attacks without tiring, and soon Alex had two more wounds, both on his legs. He had blood streaming from many spots on his body. Then, without warning, he dropped his sword and fell to the ground.

The evil figure watched in delight as he slowly put his weapons away. He would now feast on his victim as he had so many times before. He walked over to the fallen opponent and kicked him. Nothing happened. The creature eased his way to the ground and sat on his knees in front of Alex. Confidently, the monster put his hand on Alex's neck and began to squeeze. Its eyes turned to horror when it saw a silver dagger coming directly at its head. It was too late to move, and the creature knew it. The dagger struck the monster in its empty eye socket and pierced its skull.

Alex rolled over and faded into unconsciousness. His last thoughts were of how he wished he had brought one of Artimus's healing potions with him instead of giving them both to NeShae and Matthew.

The sound of the two   horses' rhythmic footsteps continued mile after mile as NeShae and Matthew continued toward their goal. "How much farther?" NeShae asked, breaking the silence. "I'm growing weary of all this riding."

"We'll be there by nightfall," Matthew answered.

"I do hope Alex is close behind us," she continued.

"I'm sure he is," Matthew responded. "I'm sure he is."

Alex awoke and looked around, confused. He had been unconscious for most of the day, for it was near dark. He tried to move his arm, but couldn't. One leg was also wounded badly, and the other was hardly any better.

He looked to where the battle had taken place and saw that his foe was still there, lying face down on the wet ground. Alex knew that he had to get up and make his way to Merquill's, for he had told Matthew and NeShae that he would be close behind them. With dried blood and wounds covering his body, Alex picked up his sword and the staff. He left the dagger where it was. He had others.

Painfully, he made his way over to his horse, who had miraculously stayed during the fight. After many tries, and with much pain, he finally got himself onto the mount's back and wearily started toward Merquill's. He rode nonstop for two days and nights until he finally had to stop to rest longer than a few minutes. His arm was still limp, but he could at least manage to walk a little now. He made a small fire and sat down beside it. He wanted to stay awake in case danger came, but he couldn't stop his exhaustion from overcoming him as he drifted into sleep.

Matthew finally started to slow his pace a little, and after another mile or so, he finally looked to NeShae and spoke, "This is it," as they rode into a cluster of trees just outside of Donaville. In the middle of the tiny forest was a lone house built halfway into a large hill.

"This is Merquill's home?" NeShae asked, perhaps expecting something a little more elaborate.

"Yup," Matthew responded. "Let's just hope he's home."

It had been five days now since King Dlemar had last eaten, and he was beginning to weaken considerably. He felt so helpless. He wished that death would just take him so that his mind wouldn't be altered by the hideous Crown.

Then he heard the door close. It was the mage. "It seems as though someone cares about you after all, Kingy," Galdon said coldly. "Three young children are searching for you now, but…"

"Who are…" Dlemar was cut short.

"Never interrupt me!" Galdon screamed as loudly as he could. Then he settled down and continued normally, "It doesn't look as though they'll be looking much longer, though." Galdon laughed as he threw his head back and closed his eyes. As soon as he finished, he looked back at the king and sarcastically continued, "My, my, Kingy, it looks as though you've lost some weight! You really should eat more; you're starting to look sickly."

King Dlemar said nothing as the mage's laughter filled the room. He was conserving his energy, waiting for the moment when he would strike.

After his brief rest, Alex continued again toward Donaville and Merquill. That very evening, Alex saw the cluster of trees that Matthew had described so perfectly to him. Although his wounds had healed some, Alex was still fatigued from his battle and the long ride. He wearily steered his horse into the woods and found what he was looking for, a stone structure built halfway into the ground. He studied it closely, looking for any hint that Matthew and NeShae had already made it here. Then he saw their horses, and his question was answered. He approached the house, still on his horse, and waited for someone to see him and to help. Only a few seconds later, the door burst open and NeShae came running out, tears rolling down her face. She helped him off the horse and looked at his bloody and injured body.

Alex looked into the eyes he thought he'd never see again and said in an obviously pain-filled voice, "I got the staff." With a small smile on his face, he closed his eyes to rest. NeShae kissed him gently, and then called for some help to bring him inside.

After they brought him into the house, they washed his wounds as he slept soundly. He rested for hours before he finally awoke and called to NeShae. She quickly appeared and gave the prince a warm loving hug.

"Well," Alex said without hesitation, "can I meet this famous Merquill we've heard so much about?"

NeShae chuckled silently to herself and said with a grin, "Sure." Then she left the room.

A few moments later, NeShae re-entered the room with Matthew and another figure behind her. NeShae stepped forward, trying to conceal the smile that was forming on her face and said, "Alex, meet Merquill the Sage."

Alex's mouth dropped open as he stared at the sage in disbelief. Still in shock, he forced himself to utter the words, "But—but you're a…"

A MUCH NEEDED FRIEND

"A woman?" her melodious voice asked as she gave him an understanding smile. "You're right; I am." As soon as she finished speaking, they all began to laugh. All of them, that is, except for Alex, who was still in shock from the sage's initial appearance. Alex studied her carefully, trying to understand how anyone in his right mind could confuse this lovely woman with a man. She stood just a few inches below six feet tall, and was very young; at least she looked like it. Her golden, flowing hair reached the middle of her back, and a cheerful smile was painted on her face.

When Alex was finally able to speak, he said, "I'm sorry, my lady; it's just that I was so sure you were a man."

"It's okay," she said softly, "and please, call me Merquilla."

"Merquilla?" Alex asked, stressing the last syllable of her

64

name.

"Yes," she answered with a small grin, "and you're not the first to make the mistake. People like the idea of a male sage better than a woman anyway. But we'll talk of that later. Right now you must rest. You have many wounds, and must give them time to heal. So close your eyes, dear prince, and we will talk later."

Her words were so gentle that Merquilla reminded Alex of his own mother, who was probably worried sick by now about both her husband and her son. Alex agreed to rest but watched as Merquilla and Matthew left the room, leaving him and NeShae alone. For the first time since Alex had arrived, NeShae finally had the chance to ask him a question. "What happened when you went back?"

Alex looked at her through his tired eyes as he gave her every last detail of the disfigured creature and his fight to the death. The thought of the creature made NeShae shiver in fear as she listened to Alex's story. When he finally finished, NeShae kissed him once again and pulled a blanket over his badly scarred limbs. She leaned gently over him and whispered in his ear, "You've been through much, my love. Sleep well." Then she turned and silently left the room to join Merquilla and Matthew.

She found the two of them outside, talking and laughing with mugs in their hands. The cool wind whistled through the surrounding trees as NeShae approached them and listened in on their conversation. Before she could say anything, however, Merquilla asked, "Does he sleep?"

"Yes," she answered in a tone that showed her obvious excitement at Alex's return. "He's lucky he even made it back, you know. He could have easily been killed trying to get that old staff back."

"Would you mind if I took a look at that old staff?" the sage asked with a chuckle.

"No, of course not," NeShae answered, hoping that Merquilla would find that it was indeed worth all of the trouble. "It's in Alex's room; I'll go get it if you want."

"That's okay; I can look at it later, when he's awake," Merquilla responded. After a short moment of silence she spoke again, "Artimus told me of the powers you have over wood and fire."

NeShae began to laugh at her statement and replied, "Well, I'd hardly call them powers. They're more like useful little gifts."

"They may be more than you think," Merquilla responded, her voice changing to a more serious tone. "Does your mother or father have any such powers?"

"I don't think so," NeShae answered, trying to recall any instances in which she had seen her parents do anything similar to her own gifts. "No, at least not that I know of."

"Why would her powers have anything to do with her parents?" asked Matthew, who had been quiet until now.

"Well, they may have nothing to do with it," Merquilla answered slowly, as if considering every word she said. "But then again, it could help prove something which would be very useful to all of you in the future."

"What would that be?" NeShae asked, intrigued by the mystery in the sage's voice.

Merquilla locked gazes with NeShae for a moment, and then answered her question. "It could prove that you do, indeed, have the powers of a druid."

Galdon waited patiently as the servant walked in and nervously told his master of the events that he had been told of.

"What?" the mage screamed as he gave the frightened servant a death-filled stare, "What do you mean, they've escaped? How? How could this happen?" His shouts filled the darkened halls of his fortress as the small grubby servant grew more and more uneasy with each passing minute. "Go tell Terrig to meet me in my chambers immediately. It's time to put my plans in motion."

"A druid?" NeShae questioned in an almost amused tone.

"But doesn't a person have to train or something to become a druid? I mean, they have such great powers, and I have only a few small gifts—how could I possibly…"

"Just calm down," Merquilla responded, trying to quiet NeShae's unending questions. "I said I'm not sure; we'll look into it later. For now, let's talk of your trip. As soon as Alex is able to travel, you must make your way toward the Blue Mountains. This is where both Artimus and I believe that Alex's father is being held. There has been much activity around the area in the last few months, and we fear that this old wizard may have kidnapped Dlemar for a reason. What it is, however, is another question. There are a number of ways to go, each involving obstacles of its own, but those too can be discussed later."

"Are you sure that King Dlemar is being held somewhere in the Blue Mountains?" Matthew asked, trying to make sure they would be heading in the right direction.

"Well, no, I'm not positive, but it's the best guess I have," she told him with a wink.

"That's good enough for me," NeShae answered, as they all smiled, each filled with their own thoughts on the journey in front of them.

"Enough talk," Merquilla said suddenly, "for NeShae and I have much work to do and many things to learn. Matthew, would you mind looking after Alex for a while?"

"No, not at all," Matthew answered, surprised at the new seriousness in the lovely sage's voice.

"Good. We'll be in my study chambers if you need us," Merquilla continued. "Come, NeShae, we have many things to accomplish and very little time."

They were almost gone. King Dlemar had been working on his ropes steadily for as long as he could remember. And it was paying off. Just a little more…he heard the door open. It was Galdon. He knew it.

"Well, well, Kingy, it seems as though your little rescuers were stronger than I thought," the mage's voice echoed in a dull sickly tone. "But no matter, we will just have to speed things up a bit. Terrig!" he yelled. "Bring the crown for our dear little Kingy."

A few moments later Dlemar felt the touch of a hand grabbing his throat. the king knew what was next; he knew that the Crown was only inches from his head. With all of his might, he gave one last desperate pull on his badly wounded bindings, and they gave. Dlemar, now seeing his chance, threw the torn ropes to the floor and drew all of the strength he had left into one upward blow aimed at the large creature in front of him. Dlemar's fist struck it in the chest, knocking the wind from it and throwing it to the ground. As the king's heart raced from his first bit of exercise in days, he knew that he still was not free. With his aching and feeble legs he tried desperately to run for the open doorway that seemed a week's travel away. His legs carried him as fast as they could, until Dlemar heard the shout of rage from the evil mage behind him. Then he felt a sundering force hit his back as he flew against the farthest wall. All he saw was blackness.

"Where's NeShae at?" Alex asked Matthew in a groggy, half-asleep voice. "Is she with Merquilla? She's not alone, is she?"

"Just calm down," Matthew answered him as he gently pushed him back to where he had been lying. "Yes, she's with Merquilla, and she's just fine." Then Matthew proceeded to tell him all about Merquilla's thoughts about NeShae having druidic powers.

Alex showed no sign of emotion, but only listened as Matthew continued his explanation of the events which had occurred while Alex was sleeping. When Matthew finally finished, he waited for a response from the prince. At last, after a few moments of silence, Alex spoke, "A druid, eh? Well, I guess that would explain a lot of things. A lot of things." Alex dropped his head back and pondered the thought of NeShae's newfound powers. "How long have they been up in her room?" Alex asked.

"I don't know, most of the day, I suppose," Matthew answered. "Why do you ask?"

"I'd just like to know what's going on up there, that's all," Alex said with a small grin, "But for right now, I have to get back on my feet. We have to get moving as soon as possible; there's no telling what kind of trouble my father is in, or even if NeShae's brother is still alive."

"But you've been through so much," Matthew reminded him in a stern voice. "Why don't you just get some more sleep and try to walk tomorrow?"

Alex gave Matthew a reassuring look that made the prince's companion do nothing but smile and shrug his shoulders. "Okay, it's your body, not mine," Matthew said as the prince began to pull himself to a sitting position.

"All right, let's try it again," the calm voice from Merquilla said. "This time let the powers flow—don't try to overpower them. Let it happen naturally."

"I'll try," NeShae said slowly, already starting to work her magic. Merquilla watched, hopeful at what might occur within the next few moments. As she did, she saw a yellow soothing light flow from the tips of NeShae's fingers and onto the large piece of wood which was on the floor in front of her. NeShae's face seemed relaxed, as did her whole body as she continued her magic. Merquilla watched intensively as the wood slowly began to move. Then, in one jerky motion, it twisted quickly in half. The entire piece of wood had changed shape. NeShae's eyes lit up as she dropped her hands and looked on in amazement at her accomplishment. She could only whisper a few short words as she stared in disbelief. "I did it."

"Yes, my dear," came the sage's soft words, "you sure did."

Dlemar opened his eyes and peered at his new environment. He was in a large, richly-decorated room with two guards standing at what appeared to be the only exit. His entire body ached, and when he looked down he could see why. The whole left side of his body was charred, evidently from an explosion—perhaps an explosion that was created by Galdon, which was why he probably fell unconscious. Dlemar tried to get up but stopped as soon as he realized the true intensity of the pain surging throughout his body. He dropped his head. He thought about where his beautiful wife was, and how worried she must be. He thought about Robin, and how pressured he must be having to deal with most of the castle business by himself. Then he thought of his son, Alex. Where was he right now? Had Artimus cured him of his maddening adolescent attitude?

Just then Dlemar heard the noise of a door shutting. He felt a cold searing pain shoot down the length of his body at the sight of the person in front of him. He saw Galdon walking toward him with a large sickly smile painted on his dirty and scarred face. When Galdon was close enough, the king drew back his head and prepared to spit directly into the mage's face. As he did, however, Dlemar noticed the weight of something resting on his head. the king questioningly raised his hands to determine what this newfound object was. It was cold, ice cold. It was the Crown.

Before Dlemar's horror could translate into words, Galdon stepped forward, looked deeply into the eyes of Dlemar's shocked face, and said mockingly, "Isn't it about time you showed some loyalty to your new master? Bow before Galdon, Kingy!"

Dlemar couldn't fight it. The Crown had taken control of his body. The king watched himself in shock and revulsion as he gently bowed to one knee and chanted, "I will do as you say, Master."

"There, see, that wasn't so hard," Alex said casually as he wobbled on his two very unsteady legs. "Now let's go see what's keeping NeShae and Merquilla." The look in Matthew's eyes told Alex that the young boy wasn't sure if Alex should be walking around yet, so Alex tried to convince him that it was the right thing to do. "It's all right; I feel fine."

"Yeah, right," was all Matthew could say, for they both knew that Alex was in just as much pain now as ever. But nevertheless, they continued up the stairs to look for NeShae and Merquilla. After a little help from Matthew, Alex finally made it to the top of the stairs, just in time to see both NeShae and Merquilla appear through a door to the left of them. Alex knew immediately from the look on NeShae's face that he was in trouble.

"What are you doing out of bed?" came her stern words. Alex opened his mouth to answer her, but was cut off immediately. "I told you to stay in bed and get some rest, so would you please do so?" She went over to him and gently grabbed his waist to help him back down the stairs. As she did so, she gave him a reassuring smile and spoke again. "Now, can I trust you two boys alone again? Or do Merquilla and I have to baby-sit the both of you?" The three of them laughed quietly at her remark and watched as Alex began to blush. They reached the bottom of the stairs and NeShae helped Alex back over to where he had been resting. Alex slowly lowered himself to his resting place and watched as everyone else prepared to leave.

Suddenly he sat up and spoke, "Wait a minute. I've had enough of this. I'm not going to rest, and I'm not going to wait until my wounds heal. My father is who knows where, and we still need to find one of those magical weapons for your brother. We can't sit here wasting time while others need our help. So I've made a decision, and we're sticking with it. We're continuing on our trip early tomorrow morning. Okay?" Alex looked to everyone, and held NeShae's gaze the longest, searching for any hint of what they were thinking.

After some hesitation, NeShae responded. "I agree," she said as a shock to everyone standing there. "I think Alex is well enough to ride, and we have to continue soon, or else everything we've worked so hard for will be lost."

Then they looked to Matthew, who had been standing quietly by himself, willing to follow any plan of action they agreed on. "What?" he spoke softly as their eyes searched him. "It doesn't matter to me what we do. I'm just along for the ride."

"Then it's settled," Alex spoke again. "We will ride tomorrow at sunrise."

Merquilla's songlike voice pierced the air as she spoke, "Then we have much to prepare for, don't we?"

King Dlemar sat quietly in the darkened room that had served as his chamber for the last few days. He tried with all of his might to remove the Crown that had so easily robbed him of what little freedom he had had left. But it was no use. It was there to stay. He searched his mind for an answer to his problem, but could find none. He turned his gaze to the same place it had been ever since he had arrived here—to the dismal mountains surrounding him.

"You must first make your way across the Drowning Sea, for I believe that both your father and the weapons you seek lie to the north, in the Blue Mountains," Merquilla spoke as everyone listened intently. "Do not pass through Tenlarick, for the folks there are very unfriendly and don't take well to strangers. Make your path more easterly, so as to avoid entering Tenlarick. Make sure you stay east of the city, and not west, for to the west lies the Forest of the, Tall, which has been a final resting place for many. A few days travel past Tenlarick is the city of Danden. You can rest at the inn there, for I know the innkeeper well. Just look for the Swirling Winds Tavern, and I'll send word of your arrival. From there you must travel due north, straight into the Blue Mountains. The mountains themselves hide many dangers, including the freezing winds that surround the desolate area night and day. So be sure to pack enough provisions and clothes for the trip. I wish I could tell you exactly where Galdon's fortress is, but I don't know, for it is a large place. Just getting there will be an achievement. I'm afraid that you'll have to rely on each other to find him once you get there." Then Merquilla looked slowly into each of the three wondering faces that were in front of her. "Do you have any questions?" she asked as they all stared at her with blank looks on their faces.

"No, I don't," Alex replied as both NeShae and Matthew also shook their heads no in response. "I think you've told us more than enough. I thank you very much, Merquilla. You truly are a wondrous sage."

"Ah, I have done little," Merquilla said. "It is you who must be the wondrous ones. For a great test lies in front of you. I give you one piece of advice, however, and heed it well. No matter what happens, stick together, for together you have a chance. Separated, you will surely fall. Now, let's get some sleep. You have got a long road in front of you tomorrow."

They all agreed immediately to Merquilla's last idea, for it had been a long day for everyone, especially NeShae. Merquilla and Matthew left the room talking to each other about the punishment for theft in Tenlarick. NeShae and Alex chuckled as their companions' voices faded into the distance, and they were left alone.

"So, what exactly happened up there this afternoon and evening?" Alex asked curiously.

"Oh, nothing," NeShae answered as she gave Alex one of her girlish smiles.

"Okay, that's fine, if you don't want to tell me…"

"It was nothing," NeShae continued. "Merquilla was just helping me with some of the powers that I was supposedly born with, that's all."

"Sure, I bet that's all," Alex laughed as he gently touched her hand with his. "Now should we get some sleep, my beautiful young druid, or should we just talk all night long?"

NeShae smiled as she watched Alex talk to her in the same cool tone that he had always used. She slowly leaned toward him and gave him a light kiss on the forehead. Lost in each other's eyes, NeShae spoke, "You're right, we had better get some sleep; morning will come quickly." At that she gave Alex one last caring glance and then stood up and strolled to the doorway. Alex continued to watch her figure leave, but stopped her exit with a few words just before she left the room. "NeShae," he said softly.

She turned around and looked deeply into his obviously adoring eyes and asked, "Yes?"

The prince's face turned into a look of nervousness as he said quietly, "I, I…"

"What is it?" NeShae asked again with a hopeful smile forming on her face.

Alex hesitated for a moment, dropped his head and in a deep voice continued, "Um, I…Thanks for taking care of my wounds."

NeShae's smile faded as she responded in a dull voice, "That's what I'm here for." After she shook her head and smiled, she turned and exited the room.

Galdon strolled cockily into the room where the king sat motionless. The mage walked steadily up to Dlemar and looked directly into the king's glossy eyes. After a few moments Galdon finally spoke. "Well, Kingy, it looks as though it's time to put my little plan into motion. Won't your kingdom be pleased to have their honorable king return to them?" Galdon laughed. "As a matter of fact, they'll probably be so pleased that they won't even notice their very own little Kingy taking advantage of them. And for what, you may ask?" Galdon continued as he paced back and forth in front of the silent king. "So they can help me take over the surrounding areas, of course. Soon, not only will I rule Terrigrin, but also the entire Drowning Sea!" Galdon's voice was mysteriously evil and insane, and Dlemar knew he was serious.

"But why?" the king asked, breaking the mage's evil thoughts. "Why do you want to rule all of that area? You already have a fortress of your own; why don't…"

"Because, you fool," Galdon interrupted harshly. "Why do you rule? Is it because you like sitting in a larger-than-normal chair every day? No! It's because of power. Power. That's what I will soon have, and more than anyone in the realms. Power."

Dlemar tried to dispute the mage again, but couldn't bring himself to do it. His thoughts were cloudy, and he couldn't think clearly. Maybe Galdon was right, Dlemar voiced inside his head. Maybe he was the right person to rule Terrigrin, and maybe he could help him do it.

The Crown glistened atop the king's head.

The light glow of the slowly forming morning sun glistened off the trees which protected the small dwelling of Merquilla's. Alex slowly opened his eyes, somehow hoping to see his father's face in front of him. But it wasn't there. Instead, there was a small fire which had dwindled down to nothing but coals during the night. The prince arose, got dressed, and began walking up the stairs to where NeShae and Matthew were sleeping. He stopped abruptly as soon as he noticed Merquilla descending the flight of stairs in front of him. He smiled lightly as he nodded and spoke. "Good morning, Merquilla. And how was your night's rest?"

"Well, fine, thank you," Merquilla replied as she reached the bottom of the stairs and stood next to the prince. "I've already wakened NeShae and Matthew. They should be down soon."

"I was just on my way to do that myself, but since I don't have to, perhaps we can talk ourselves, before the others come," Alex said in a serious voice.

"Well, of course," Merquilla answered. "What's on your mind?"

"I've been thinking of our trip," Alex started. "Merquilla, I want you to tell me the absolute truth about something."

"I'll do my best," she answered, wondering what was troubling Alex so much. "What is it?"

"Well, what do you think our chances are? I mean, is this Galdon guy too powerful for us? And what about NeShae and Matthew? I don't want anything to happen to either one of them. I was wondering if I should…maybe I should do this on my own, so that no one else gets hurt."

"Oh, my dear prince," Merquilla said in a quiet motherly tone. "What has happened to your spark? Your never-die attitude? Don't give up hope, for without hope, there is nothing left. Only a world of bitter strangers. Without your companions, you will surely fail in your task. And if you are worried about bringing them against their will, don't be, for NeShae has just as much of a reason to be here as you. As for Matthew, well, he has nowhere else to be. You have given him something to live for. You have given him hope. Now give up these silly thoughts and continue your journey as you have intended all along."

Alex's face turned to a look of agreement as Merquilla spoke her last few words. "You're right," he said quietly.

"Good morning, my prince," came a voice from the stairs. Alex's head turned to meet the lovely gaze of NeShae. Never before had he seen her so radiant, so hopeful, so ready. Behind her came Matthew, who also greeted the prince, although Alex was still so awe-struck at NeShae's beauty that he hardly even noticed.

"Good morning, NeShae," Alex returned as he gently lifted her hand and kissed it. "How did you sleep?"

"Just fine," NeShae continued. "Merquilla's beds are of the best quality I have ever slept in. How about you?"

"I slept well also, but we mustn't continue our talk of sleep. We have to get an early start to make up for our lost time. Do you have everything, NeShae?" Alex asked, and watched as NeShae nodded her head yes. "How about you, Matthew?"

"Sure do," Matthew said enthusiastically, obviously excited to continue on this journey of theirs.

"Good, then why don't we get going before the sun sets again," Alex said as everyone laughed. The four of them looked at each other, each of them not knowing what to say next, until Alex finally broke the silence and said, "Merquilla, I thank you for everything, and if…when we return, I will make sure that you are rewarded for all of the generosity that you have shown us. We never could have made it this far without you." At that, Alex gave the sage a warm hug, and made his way out the door.

Matthew was next, and with teary eyes he spoke, "Thank you for everything, Merquilla. You've been great to all of us, especially me. I feel like you're my own mother, the mother I can hardly remember. Thanks." Then he concluded by giving her a hug and walking toward the door. Just as he was about to exit, Merquilla said, "You're always welcome here, all of you."

NeShae and Merquilla were now alone, and they stood silently as they watched each other, neither knowing exactly what to say. Then Merquilla started, "My dear, you have learned well, and you will continue to learn if only you continue to try. Here, take this book, study it every night, and it will help you progress even more. And remember, you must believe in yourself, and you will succeed."

NeShae, whose tears were already forming took the old worn book from Merquilla's hands and spoke, "Thank you, Merquilla, for everything—for helping Alex, for being so kind to all of us, for giving Matthew the love he needs, and for helping me to find what I may have been looking for for so many years. Thank you."

"You're welcome, my dear. You're welcome." The two of them embraced each other and hugged for a few moments before they heard a voice from outside yell, "We'd like to start this year sometime, NeShae!"

"That must mean I should get going," NeShae said as they parted and she wiped the tears from her eyes. "Good-bye, Merquilla."

"Good-bye, NeShae, till we meet again soon," Merquilla answered as NeShae exited the building and found Alex and Matthew waiting on their horses.

"Okay, okay, I'm coming," she said as she mounted her horse. The three of them waved to Merquilla, who was watching from a large window, and made their way out of the safe shelter of Merquilla's home.

Merquilla turned her head to the bird that was sitting in the tree right outside her open window. "Well, my friend, you can return to Artimus and tell him that all is well; they are continuing their journey as planned."

Ptilon immediately took to flight and started off across the blue hazy sky. Merquilla watched as the majestic bird climbed higher and higher into the morning air, and looked back to the companions whom she hoped would be all right. She thought of how wonderful it had been to have their company, and she smiled.

"Where should we try to cross the Drowning Sea, Alex?" NeShae asked as they continued their journey on horseback. It was approaching noon and the companions could already clearly see the town of Donaville in the distance.

"I think we should stay out of Donaville if possible. Who knows what kind of trouble is waiting for us there," Alex answered, still looking at the outline of the enormous city. "Perhaps we can find someone to take us across just outside the city, along the shore."

"I agree," Matthew spoke up. "I've heard some pretty bad tales about life in Donaville, and I don't want to be tellin' stories of my own."

"Then let's make our way to the west of the city," Alex said. "And maybe we can find some help there."

"How does this sound, Kingy?" Galdon asked as he began to read the letter aloud:

To the kingdom of Terrigrin:

It seems as though I have mistakenly found your dear and lovely King Dlemar, and though I would usually gladly bring him to you for nothing, I am in a particularly nasty mood at this time. So if you would like to see your king's scowling face again, please send 10,000 silver pieces immediately.

Allies Indeed,
G

"Ten thousand silver pieces?" Dlemar asked questioningly. "Is that all I'm worth?"

"Well, I don't want to take the chance of them not wanting you back, you fool," the mage shouted back at him. "We have to get you back to the castle so that we can begin our conquest together!" There was a short pause before Galdon hollered again, "Messenger!"

"Yes, my lord," a quiet voice answered as a small grungy boy entered the room almost before Galdon's voice had died down.

"I want you to take this letter immediately to the kingdom of Terrigrin. It is of utmost importance, and it must be carried out to perfection. I am giving you a magical steed that will allow you to travel there in a fraction of the normal time. Do you understand?"

"Yes, my lord, I will do as you say," came the boy's monotone reply.

"Good," Galdon answered, "then be on your way."

As Dlemar listened to their conversation he couldn't help but think about what he was doing. His wife and son. His guards. The castle. It was so foggy.

"What about that boathouse over there?" NeShae asked as the three of them made their way past the randomly placed buildings along the shoreline of the Drowning Sea.

"Why not? I guess we have to start somewhere," Alex answered as they started to make their way toward the small black shape of a boathouse in the distance under the darkening evening sky. Soon they were standing in front of the doorway which led into the run down boathouse. Alex looked cautiously around before he finally put his right hand on the hilt of his sword, then knocked with his other. Immediately the door opened to reveal a young woman, perhaps in her twenties, who looked questioningly to all three of them.

"What do you want?" the woman asked sheepishly as she left the door open only a crack.

"We would like to speak to someone about a ride across the Drowning Sea, to the other side of The Neck," Alex answered abruptly. "Can you be of service to us, good woman?"

"Of course," she spoke softly as she opened the door fully and motioned for them to come in. "My name is Abrina. I will go get my husband, Russell; maybe he can help you." She turned and walked into the back room, leaving the three companions alone and wondering. She soon returned with another figure, a man who looked only a few years older than herself. He was muscular with an unshaven face, and wore a torn blue shirt with matching pants. The smile on his face was comforting to the party as they looked at him through wondering eyes.

"Please come and sit," the man said in a loud deep voice as he motioned for the party to enter the building.

"My name is Alex," the prince said as all three of them made their way slowly into the small house. "We are here on urgent business and need a way across the Drowning Sea as soon as possible. Is there any way you can help us?"

"Why, of course, that's my job!" the man laughed ferociously. "But for a fee, you understand? Say fifty silver pieces?"

"Fifty silver pi..." Matthew started but was cut off by Alex.

"Done," Alex stated without a thought as he pulled a small coin bag from within his clothing, "but we leave now."

"It's a deal," Russell said as he gave his wife a cheerful smile. "Let's go."

The three of them excitedly followed Russell out of the boathouse as he led them down toward what appeared to be the docks. "What about our horses?" Matthew asked as they continued toward the shoreline.

"Don't worry about them," Russell reassured him. "There are some stables close by where Abrina can keep them until you return." They continued on until Russell finally said, "Well, here we are." The party looked up to see the shape of a medium-sized ship which appeared to be in almost perfect condition. "What do you think?"

"If it gets us there, I think it's great," Alex said as he started to climb the plank which led on to the vessel.

NeShae, trying to cover for what she thought was Alex's rudeness, politely said, "It looks very lovely, Russell. I'm sure it's a wonderful ship, indeed."

"We'd better get going before Alex leaves without us," Russell continued as he, NeShae, and Matthew followed Alex up the plank and onto the ship. On board they saw what appeared to be other sailors who were carrying crates from one location to another. As soon as the party reached the top of the plank, the other men stopped their work and slowly made their way closer to were NeShae, Alex, Matthew, and Russell were standing.

"I think I've found us some good ones this time, boys," Russell shouted as he gave a loud roar of laughter. "Let's get 'em!" he screamed as the other sailors drew their swords and ran screaming toward the party.

Alex was the first to react, as he grabbed his bow and sent a fiery arrow ripping through the body of one of the sailors and into the water beyond. Matthew ducked quietly into the shadows of the ship's cover and waited silently until one of the unsuspecting sailors came running too close to him and met his end. NeShae immediately held out her staff and began chanting some arcane words which were unfamiliar to all those around her. She watched excitedly as the boards in front of the pursuing sailors snapped viciously up, slamming into their bodies and knocking them to the deck. Alex repeatedly fired arrow after arrow into the bodies of the sailors, and soon only one was left, Russell. Alex looked at him with a stare of death and said in a cold tone, "Now, take us across the Drowning Sea."

Russell didn't hesitate for a moment, but instead walked slowly to the ship's wheel and asked, "But what about the sailors? We have no one to man the ship. And it's dark. How can we possibly start out when it's pitch black?"

With lightning-quick reflexes, Alex drew his sword in his empty hand and touched the sweaty neck of the captain. "We go now," Alex whispered in Russell's ear, then turned and walked to the main sail to help Matthew raise it. Russell, who was now trembling with fear, walked quickly over to another part of the ship and began preparing it for use. After a short time, they released the ropes and slowly made their way out of the shelter of the small bay which they were in. They were finally on their way across the Drowning Sea.

"How long do you think it will take?" Matthew asked Russell as soon as they had raised the sails. They were standing there alone, as NeShae and Alex were busy preparing something to eat.

"We should be there by tomorrow evening," Russell said as he looked around nervously. "Hey, kid," Russell spoke quietly, "why don't we get rid of the other two, and we can split their treasure up? It'll be me and you, partners—what do ya say?"

Matthew looked at the man carefully, taking note of every feature on him, then drew his long silver dagger and laughed softly, "Why do I need their treasure when I already have yours?" Matthew then held up the small brown pouch that obviously had belonged to Russell just a short time ago.

"Why, you little thief!" Russell screamed as he lunged forward. Matthew's quickness proved superior, as the captain missed Matthew completely and crashed to the deck. In the blink of an eye, Matthew's dagger point came to rest on the skin of Russell's neck. By this time, NeShae and Alex had appeared from below deck because of the noise. Alex only grinned as he watched Matthew teasingly shake his finger at Russell. Then Matthew helped the very ungracious captain up and they continued as if nothing had happened. Alex and NeShae made their way back down below to where they had almost finished preparing some food.

As they continued fixing their meal, NeShae slowly looked up at Alex, who was busy cutting some meat. After debating for quite some time, she finally spoke, "Alex, how do you feel about me?"

Alex looked up with a confused look on his face as he asked, "What do you mean?"

"I mean how do you feel about me?" she continued. "Do you like my company, or do you have the urge to throw up every time I'm near?"

"You know I love your company," Alex said as he lowered his head again and his face began to turn a deep red.

NeShae stopped what she was doing and walked gracefully over to where the prince was working in the small wooden room. She touched his hand gently with hers and looked directly into his obviously embarrassed face. "How much do you love my company?" she asked as they both leaned closer to each other.

The prince felt her golden blonde hair in his free hand as he slowly moved his head closer to hers. "Very much…"

"Is the food almost ready?" came a shout from the door on top of the stairs which led down into the room that Alex and NeShae were in. Immediately they parted as both of them took in a few deep breaths before NeShae finally answered, "Yes, we'll be up in a moment, Matthew." Alex and NeShae gave each other one last look, then Alex took NeShae's tender hand and brought it to his lips. He kissed it. She looked at the prince with gentle loving eyes as they once again parted and brought the food up.

"It's about time," Matthew said sarcastically as soon as they appeared. "Did you have to grow the food down there or what?" he asked as he gave the prince a small wink that he hoped NeShae did not notice. "I'm starved; let's eat."

All of them, even Russell, sat down and enjoyed the meal that Alex and NeShae had prepared. As they were sitting there, Matthew's eye caught a light off in the distance, which appeared to be moving. "Alex," he said softly, "what do you think that light is? It kind of looks like it might be another boat."

Alex turned his head to the place that Matthew was motioning to and peered into the darkness. After a moment, he spoke, "I think you're right; it does look like a boat. I think I can make out three lights, not one. Any ideas as to what it means?"

A smile appeared on Russell's face as he said, "They are friends of mine, and as for the three torches, they mean that you are in deep trouble. The three lights stand for pain, death, and destruction." Alex stared at the distant lights and thought.

"No, you fool!" Galdon screamed at Dlemar at the top of his lungs. "You have to be more convincing than that. The entire kingdom has to believe that you are the same old Kingy, do you understand?" Dlemar nodded his head as if he understood. "Why couldn't you have just let me put on the stupid Crown so that the effects would have taken over completely by now, you stubborn fool?" the king shrugged his shoulders as if he did not fully understand the question. Galdon continued, "Perhaps we should wait to rehearse the speech until the effects of the Crown are at their peak." Dlemar nodded. He understood completely.

Alex stood up and grabbed Russell by the shirt. "Have you set us up?" he screamed into the man's ear. "Are we even headed in the right direction?" Alex threw the captain back, jumped up, and walked to the side of the ship. He stared closely at the lights, which appeared to be getting closer, but whether they were or not he was not sure. In a sudden burst of energy, Alex grabbed his sword from its scabbard and ran back to Russell. "You dirty traitor!" he yelled as loud as he could into the silent night. Then a calm look came over his face as he looked back to Russell and began speaking again. "It is not going to end like this, my foolish friend. And if you think you are going to be rescued, think again, for if I for one moment believe that we are going to be captured, I will cut your throat and let the creatures of the sea deal with your vile body. Got it?" Russell nodded his head, indicating that he did, indeed, understand the prince. "Now, we haven't got much time. We need to do something quickly before their ship gets too close."

"How about praying?" Russell grinned. Alex, who was filled with a rage already caused by this man, could not stop himself from swinging the hilt of his sword upward into the jaw of the captain. Alex watched as Russell fell to the deck, but felt more comfortable when NeShae examined him, then said, "He's only unconscious."

"What can we do?" Matthew asked in a semi-desperate tone.

"Don't worry," Alex answered, his voice showing that he had calmed down. "We'll be okay. We just need to buy some time, that's all. Now, do you think he has us headed in the right direction?"

"Yeah, I think so. I was here the whole time," Matthew said after he thought about the question.

"Good, then let's start by seeing what kind of supplies we have to work with. Matthew, you douse all the flames. NeShae and I will go see what we can find down below."

Matthew agreed and quickly went to work. Alex and NeShae started by tying up Russell, then continued by making their way down below deck, to where they could hopefully find something that could help them. As they searched cabinets, drawers, and chests, they both realized that they weren't going to find anything of use. This was a passenger ship, not a war vessel. Both of them soon sat down next to each other, each of them trying to come up with an idea.

Alex finally broke the silence by saying, "Wait a minute; what about your robe? Didn't we find a raft or something on one of the patches?" Both of them immediately looked to NeShae's cloak and it didn't take long before NeShae pointed out a small square patch on her left shoulder which was in the shape of a wooden raft.

"But we certainly can't drift to the other side of the Drowning Sea," NeShae said to Alex, who was pondering their next move.

"You're right," he answered her, "but if we can buy enough time to get close to shore, we can use that to get to safety."

"But we're a day's travel from the other side. How can we possibly buy ourselves that much time?" NeShae asked.

"I'm leaving that up to you," Alex answered her in a voice that had started to show some sign of hope. "You must have some kind of magic in that book that Merquilla gave you that can help us…"

"The book!" NeShae shouted excitedly. "Of course, I forgot all about it! Give me some time and I'll see what I can find."

"Well, try not to take too much time," Alex stated as he started walking up the stairs which led to the upper deck. He closed the door behind him, leaving NeShae alone to study.

"Did you find anything?" Matthew asked as soon as Alex appeared from below.

"No, I'm afraid I didn't, but NeShae is still looking, and hopefully she will," Alex answered him with a tiny hint of a grin. Matthew gave him a puzzled look but pressed the issue no more. The two of them looked to the water behind them, to where their pursuers were, and noticed that the lights had appeared to get closer.

"How much time do you think we have?" Matthew asked the prince.

"Probably until about noon before they get within weapon range," Alex answered him as he continued to stare at the three lone lights in the darkness. He suddenly broke off his gaze and continued, "Dawn will be here soon, and we must be prepared to catch every morning wind possible. We must try to buy ourselves some more time in order to make it to land safely. At least there we have a fighting chance. On the water, unarmed, against a warship, the odds aren't so good, so let's check those sails again to make sure they're ready for the dawn's early winds." As they were doing this, they heard Russell's groggy voice and knew that he had awakened. Alex told Matthew to continue, then walked over to where the captain was tied up. The prince lowered himself to one knee and looked at Russell face to face.

"You've caused my party and I a lot of problems," Alex started as he stared at the captain without blinking. "If something happens to either NeShae or Matthew, I swear on my father's life, I'll kill you. This whole thing is your fault, and somehow you'll pay—if not by me, then by yourself." Russell looked at him questioningly but said nothing, for he didn't want to make the prince any angrier than he already was. Instead he dropped his head and continued to look at the ropes that held him captive. Alex left Russell to his thoughts and went over to the side of the ship and sat down to catch what little sleep he could before dawn came.

"Alex," Matthew said slowly, "Alex, the wind has already started to pick up." Alex quickly opened his eyes and got to his feet. The morning light was starting to peek through the gray haze of the early hour. The prince understood Matthew's statement, for he could already tell that the wind had picked up a considerable amount. Alex looked behind them to the other ship that had stayed about the same distance away since the last time he looked. Or so it appeared.

"Then let's get as much speed as we can," Alex told him as he walked to the main sail. "Have you seen NeShae lately?"

"No, I haven't," Matthew answered him in a worried voice, "Do you want me to go down and check on her?"

"No," Alex answered him. "She needs to be left alone. I just hope that she's found something by now, and that she can use it to help us." Russell watched as Alex and Matthew made their way around the ship, tightening ropes and positioning sails for the best results. He also knew that it would not be long before the pursuers were close enough to fire at them. They waited, making small adjustments here and there, hoping to improve their ship's speed.

After a while, Matthew spoke, "Alex, I think I can see the other side, over there," as he pointed to what was obviously the land that they had been searching for. Matthew looked back to the ship that was hunting them, and immediately knew that they had come even closer. They could now see the three lights very clearly, even in the morning light. They appeared to be large fires built right on the ship.

All that was left to do was to wait, and they did. They

waited for a few hours, and there was still no sign of NeShae. Alex was starting to become concerned but didn't want to show it in front of Matthew, so instead told him, "I'm sure NeShae will be up soon; she told me that she would be watching, and would come out when the time was right. Evidently the time isn't right." Alex felt bad about lying to Matthew, but knew that if he told him the truth he might panic.

Another hour passed and the ship gained on them even faster than they had predicted. They could easily make out the individuals on the ship, and knew that they were outnumbered by many more than they had expected. Alex knew that the ship would be close enough to fire within the hour. The prince walked calmly over to the edge of the ship and peered at the enemies who were so easily gaining on them. As he watched the gentle motion of the waves his thoughts wandered. "How could I have done this to them?" he asked himself quietly. "They've risked their lives for me, and now we sit like targets, hoping for a merciful death." Alex's head lowered and his eyes closed as he tried desperately to come up with any plan that might help them or give them the slightest chance. He remembered his mother's words when he was a small boy: "Now, Alexander, you be careful, and don't run too far into the woods." If only my mother's comforting voice were with me now, he thought to himself. "If only I knew what to do," Alex said as he raised his head to Matthew's voice.

"NeShae!" Matthew shouted excitedly. "Have you found anything that could help us in your book?"

"Well," NeShae answered him in a not-so-sure voice, "I hope so."

Alex walked calmly over to where NeShae and Matthew were standing and asked, "What have you found?"

NeShae turned to him and slowly said, "Wind." Then she turned, walked over to the side of the ship, and looked to where their followers were. She very gracefully brought her staff up and held it in the air with one arm. The other three, including Russell, watched, none of them knowing exactly what to expect. NeShae started chanting phrases that sounded very unfamiliar to all of them, but they continued to watch, almost in trances. She continued chanting, her voice becoming deeper and more powerful with each fluid sound. Her voice kept in rhythm for what seemed like hours for Alex and Matthew, and soon they realized what was happening. The wind had picked up. It was a considerable amount too, for their sails were now full, and they immediately recognized their gain in speed. NeShae's voice continued as Alex and Matthew broke off their stares and went to adjust the ship's sails in order to make full use of their newfound companion, the wind. Their hearts became hopeful as they watched their goal get closer and closer to them. The speed of their vessel had nearly doubled and they knew it wouldn't be long before they reached: land.

Alex watched curiously as NeShae continued to work her magic and noticed the effects that the spell was having on her. He could tell that it was draining her, for it appeared to be a struggle for her just to remain standing. The shoreline came even closer, and the prince looked back to see where their pursuers were. They weren't as close as before, but they were still close enough to worry about. Alex knew that they had to escape quickly when they reached the shore; otherwise, they would be caught.

"Matthew," Alex called, trying not to disturb NeShae, "Go get some rope and bring it to the main mast. I'll meet you there in a moment." He watched as Matthew unquestioningly carried out his orders and then made his way over to where Russell was sitting, still in amazement over NeShae's powers. Alex looked didn't even look at him, but instead watched the ship that was following them as he asked Russell, "Do you really think they care about you? Do you really think that they're wasting their time chasing us for your miserable life?" Russell said nothing and only listened as the prince continued his speech. "If you believe that they are, indeed, so loyal, then you will have a chance to prove it, my friend, and then we will see what the word friend truly means."

"You will see!" Russell shouted at Alex. "You will all see! And you will pay!" Alex answered him by grabbing his arm and dragging him to where the main mast was. Matthew was already there waiting for him the with rope. Alex said nothing, but pulled Russell, who was swinging his legs wildly, up against the mast and wrapped the rope several times around him. Matthew watched as the prince tied several large knots around Russell's hands, feet, and waist, and then made sure that it was all secure. Alex looked up and noticed that they were almost close enough to use NeShae's raft to get to land. He noticed that NeShae realized this too, for she suddenly stopped her chanting and sank slowly to the wooden deck of the ship, too tired to even move. The prince immediately rushed to her side and grabbed her limp body.

"NeShae," Alex said as she slowly opened her eyes, "NeShae, I know you are weak, but I need one more favor from you."

"What is it?" she asked quietly, and in a sick-sounding voice.

Alex reached to NeShae's shoulder, to where he remembered the raft patch was, and grabbed it. He watched as it quickly took form, and then told NeShae, "I need you to start the ship on fire."

NeShae didn't argue, but slowly moved her staff to the wooden deck. After mumbling some foreign words, she slowly closed her eyes. Alex watched as a small flame appeared where the staff had been, and began to grow. Before long it was a medium-sized fire. "Let's go, before it gets too large," Alex said to Matthew as he started to carry NeShae to the edge of the ship.

"But what about Russell?" Matthew asked as he looked at the captain, who had started screaming for his life just a few seconds earlier. His voice haunted both Alex and Matthew, but Alex looked sternly back to Matthew and said, "If his friends care as much as he thinks they do, then he will be safe." Then Alex motioned for Matthew to throw the raft over the side of the ship. Matthew slowly made his way down a rope which led to the surface of the water and the waiting raft. Matthew watched as Alex did the same, with NeShae held firmly in his arms. As soon as they were on the raft, they began paddling with some extra oars which they had made from some wood on board the ship. They watched as their pursuers made their way closer and closer to the burning ship and listened as Russell's terror-filled screams filled the air.

Alex looked to Matthew, who was still listening to their old captain's shrill voice, and tried to comfort him. "He'll be all right, Matthew; I'm sure they'll stop to help him, which will give us plenty of time to get out of here."

Matthew said nothing, but kept on paddling, until they reached the shoreline. The companions, with Alex still carrying NeShae, quickly exited their raft and turned to watch the ensuing ship. It came closer and closer to the burning obstacle which was in its way. The party watched carefully as the men on the ship shouted and pointed to the man who was tied helplessly to the mast. Then they changed direction and sailed around it. Alex's mouth nearly dropped open as he watched the ship change its course so that it headed directly for them.

Matthew immediately panicked as he asked nervously, "Now what do we do, Alex? It won't be long before they reach the shore, and NeShae's injured, and we don't have any horses…"

"Calm down!" Alex said sternly, trying to bring Matthew back to reality. "First of all, we have to get out of here, so let's go." Alex and Matthew looked around, searching for any shelter that might be near. In the distance they saw a large wooded area, and decided to make their way toward it. They started running, but Alex saw Matthew stop for a moment and listen. He still heard the screams of Russell from on board the burning ship.

"We have to do something, Alex," Matthew pleaded with him as tears filled his young eyes. "We can't just let him die like that, even if he is an enemy."

Alex gently set NeShae down and started to think of what they could possibly do that could help right now. Then it hit him. Artimus. He remembered when the old elf first gave him his bow. He remembered when he first shot it completely through a tree. Alex quickly pulled the magical bow from his back and looked to Matthew with a reassuring smile. The prince looked to the burning vessel, which was still fairly close to them, and found Russell, who was screaming in terror in his bonds. Alex gracefully drew the glistening string back and watched as an arrow appeared. He aimed carefully, and let go. It soared smoothly through the smoke-filled air, and struck the mast exactly where he had intended, just inches above Russell's bound body. The arrow ripped completely through the wood, and Alex watched as the mast slowly leaned to one side. The weight of its top soon carried it crashing to the water below, leaving only a stump of wood. Russell, who was more surprised than anyone, quickly pulled his ropes over the stump to free himself, and then looked to the maker of this newfound hope. He and Alex stared at each other, each of them finding a new respect for one another, as Russell held his left hand straight out, a symbol of friendship. After one final glance, Russell dove overboard safely into the water, and disappeared. Alex picked up NeShae again, and started running toward the trees that had become their next destination. Matthew followed closely behind as they ran as fast as they could.

After a few moments of running, they reached the edge of the woods and stopped to rest. They looked back to see where their pursuers were, and noticed that they had already started making their way to shore in smaller boats. Alex knew they couldn't outrun them with NeShae in the condition she was.

"Well," Alex started after a moment of hesitation, "we've got a couple of options. Either we make a run for it, and hopefully we lose them in the woods, or we make a stand right here."

Matthew looked to him for the right answer, but knew that there probably wasn't one, so he said, "How badly do you think they outnumber us?"

"Probably at least five to one," Alex said, although he knew that it could easily be much more than that.

"Just the way we like it, right?" Matthew said with a smile, as he looked to Alex for approval.

"Right," Alex answered him with a smile of his own as he now noticed that some of the men had reached the shoreline. The prince carried NeShae to a spot behind some trees and covered her unconscious body with leaves and twigs. He hoped that even if something did happen to them, NeShae still might escape safely if they didn't find her. Then he turned and walked back to where Matthew was sitting motionless.

"Seventeen," Matthew said calmly, "plus the captain and two others still on their ship." They both watched as the men waited patiently for everyone to make it to shore before they came after them.

"Matthew," Alex said suddenly as he pointed to a nearby limb, "I want you to climb that tree and wait until one of them is directly under you, and then I want you to attack. I don't want you to do anything until they're directly under you, do you understand?"

"Yes, but what about you?" Matthew asked him in a concerned tone. "Where are you going to be?"

"Right below you," Alex answered. "Now go quickly, before they get close enough to see us." Matthew obeyed immediately, and climbed the tree smoothly and silently, as he was told. He sat on one of the branches and waited to see exactly what Alex was going to do. The men had already started making their way toward the woods at quite a fast rate. Then Alex removed the bow from his shoulder and carefully lifted it with one arm and placed his other hand on the string. In a soft fluid motion he gently pulled the string back near his chin and released it. The magical arrow tore through one of the marching men and dropped him to the ground, dead. The other men looked frantically around, weapons drawn, for their invisible foe, but found none. Instead, they only watched as another arrow took the life from one of their unsuspecting comrades. And another. And another. Soon the men were running in mass confusion in the direction of the woods. Closer they came as more of them tasted the arrows of death. It didn't take long before they reached the edge of the woods, and Alex had to abandon his dear and close ally, his bow. Instead he drew his sword and made the first person who came too close to him pay dearly. Another man charged him but quickly found the same fate, as the blade of the prince's sword entered his stomach and appeared again out his back. As Alex was pulling his weapon from the dead man's body, he heard a noise and spun around to meet a large man dressed in leather armor. Behind this man and somewhat to the right was another man who had drawn a bow and was just about ready to let an arrow soar in the direction of Alex, when the prince saw a figure come crashing down on him from above. It was Matthew, and he watched from the corner of his eye as the young boy quickly finished off the archer and smiled a "You're welcome" to Alex. the prince stood still as the man in front of him charged in blind rage, but moved quickly to the side, just before contact, and watched as the man fell to the ground on his own blade.

Matthew snuck silently behind another man who was looking around for his companions, and slit his throat with ease. Alex stopped another man's hopes of success, and before long only two men stood, a prince and a young boy. They looked at each other, then at the seventeen motionless bodies that surrounded them, then they rested. After a few moments, Alex went over to where he had left NeShae and found that she had awakened during the battle and was sitting up, looking at him through confused eyes. Alex embraced her tenderly as he asked, "Are you okay?"

"I'm fine," NeShae muttered in a groggy voice, "but where are we? And has anything happened since I passed out?"

"As for where we are," Alex answered her in a caring voice, "we are safe, and that is all that matters."

Then Matthew approached them and came over to NeShae's side. "You did a great job, NeShae," he told her as he kneeled down to look at her tired face. "We never could have done it without you."

"He's right," Alex agreed as he held NeShae's hand in his.

"None of us could have done it alone." The three of them looked carefully into each other's eyes, almost as though they could feel each other's emotions. Then they held each others hands and quietly chanted, "Together we stand."

WOODED ALLIES

Galdon paced stiffly back and forth in front of the tall darkened mirror that stood before him. He watched his reflection as he carefully carried out his every thought and action. "Larrin," he shouted without a hint of warning. Within seconds the huge bulking warrior answered his master's call and entered the doorway to join him.

"What is it, my lord?" Larrin asked obediently.

"Have you heard anything from the messenger yet?" Galdon asked him in an obviously angery voice.

"No, my lord, but it has only been a few days since he left, and..." the warrior was cut off.

"Don't you think I know that, you fool?" the mage screamed. Then Galdon quickly calmed, and in a mellow tone said again, "The steed I sent him on can ride steady for weeks, needs no food or water, and can travel on water as well as land. He should be here soon. When he arrives, send him here immediately."

"Yes, my lord," Larrin answered and then left the room.

Galdon was left alone in the room. He looked to the mirror again and said confidently, "Your intelligence, my dear mage, will surely give you the kingdom that you deserve." Then he laughed.

Alex watched the night carefully as the stars shone brightly around him and his sleeping companions. They had decided to spend the night in the same spot where they had defeated the sailors just hours earlier. Alex insisted that he take the first shift and promised that he would wake the others as soon as it was their turn. He saw how soundly both of them were sleeping, however, and decided not to wake them until it was time to leave. Dawn was approaching quickly. He watched NeShae's beautiful form as her breathing rhythmically moved her body. He stared at her for a long time before he finally approached her. Without removing his eyes from her lovely, innocent face, he touched her hand and whispered softly, "NeShae, you have touched me as no one else ever has. I feel alive when I am with you, and you understand me as no one else does. I love you." Then he touched his lips to her cheek, stood up, and walked to where he had been before, underneath the shelter of a tall pine.

The sun soon started to peek through the grayish morning, and after Alex had started a small fire to make breakfast over, he went over to NeShae and Matthew and woke them from their temporary safe spots.

Matthew looked around questioningly before he said in an almost angry tone, "It's already dawn? Why didn't you wake us for our shifts?"

"You mean you wanted to take a shift, too?" Alex responded sarcastically. "I'll have to remember that next time." Matthew only smiled and shook his head. "How are you this morning, my lovely lady?" Alex asked NeShae as she began to stir.

"Just fine," she said in an obviously weary voice, "but you must be tired after staying up the entire night. Why don't we wait for a couple of hours so that you can get some sleep before we go?"

Alex gave her a grin that answered her question with a definite no, and then went to their supplies to get some food for breakfast. It wasn't long before all three of them had finished eating, when Matthew asked, "Do you think Russell is all right, Alex?"

Alex looked to Matthew, who was distraught at the thought of their previous situation with the captain. Then he answered, "He's the captain of a ship, and I'm sure he can swim like a fish. He'll be fine." Matthew looked to the spot where their old ship had been, but found only scattered boards and debris floating in the water after it had burned. Alex broke his thoughts though with his voice. "It's time we get going; the sun is already visible, and today we must make good time." NeShae and Matthew didn't argue, but instead started packing their belongings for the journey ahead.

"I hope there's a small village or town closeby where we can get some horses," Matthew said as he continued gathering his things.

"So do I," NeShae agreed, and then looked to Alex as though she wanted to know what he was thinking.

"I think we'll head northeast, until we can put the city of Tenlarick off in the distance to our left. Then we will continue due north until we reach the road going to Danden, if there is one. Does that sound okay to everyone?"

"Sounds fine to me," NeShae answered as Matthew, too, nodded his head, agreeing with them both.

"Then let's go," Alex continued, "for the day doesn't grow any longer." The party set out on foot, putting the sun in front of them and to the right. The area they were traveling in was mostly barren, with clumps of woods scattered about randomly. Around noon they stopped to have lunch, but quickly continued on their way, each of them wanting to get where they were going for different reasons. Without their horses, they made very poor time, which disappointed them, but they knew that in order to succeed, they had to travel on, no matter how long it took them. As evening approached, they saw another wooded area in front of them which they all decided would be the best place to spend the night. After about an hour of travel, they reached the edge of the trees and started to build their camp.

As NeShae started a small fire she said to Alex, "Tonight we will take turns on watch. You will not do it alone, do you understand?"

It was all Alex could do to stop himself from bursting into laughter from NeShae's demanding, motherly show, and instead he said with only a hint of a smile, "Yes, my dear," and then walked over to get some food for their supper.

Out of the corner of his eye, Alex caught a glimpse of something which startled him. He motioned to both NeShae and Matthew that something was watching them as he slowly pulled the bow from his back. NeShae stood up and peered into the dense patch of trees as Matthew drew his sword and silently made his way over to Alex. Then they saw another movement, this time behind them, and yet another from a different direction. Alex wasn't sure what to do, when all of a sudden, a tall figure appeared from within the woods. The form was dressed in a sagging brown robe and had a hood drawn, which concealed its face. The three companions watched hesitantly as the figure approached them. Alex still had his bow ready, as did Matthew his sword, but they both stood still as the figure reached them and then lowered the hood from his face. It was an older man with graying hair and a short, well-kept beard. His eyes were dark brown and looked as though they kept many secrets, and the wrinkles on his face showed time's marks.

He looked into each of the companions' faces before he finally said in a low, but almost song-filled voice, "I am Ethen, druid and keeper of these woods, and these are my companions." At that, many more figures started appearing from the woods, until there were at least thirty or forty brown-robed figures standing in front of the party. Then Ethen continued, "I know not who you are, but I would like to. Who are you, and what brings you here?"

"But the army is getting restless, my lord," came a reply from the commander who was talking privately to Galdon.

"Tell them it won't be much longer, perhaps a month. I need time to safely secure the kingdom of Terrigrin before we can start to conquer the neighboring kingdoms," Galdon answered him. "I didn't plan on that old Kingy being such a nuisance."

"What should I tell the army?" the commander asked Galdon and waited for a response.

"Tell them whatever it takes, you idiot!" Galdon screamed, "I don't care what you tell them, just make sure they are ready when it is time–do I make myself clear?"

"Yes, my lord," the commander answered.

"Good, now get out of my sight," Galdon said evilly as he turned around and looked out the window. "Soon I will be ready. Oh, but so soon."

NeShae was the first of the three to respond by answering politely, "My friend, we are here on urgent business regarding the king of Terrigrin. This is his son, Prince Alexander Denmoore. This is Matthew," she continued as she pointed to Matthew and as Alex and Matthew watched, not quite knowing what was to come next, "and I am NeShae. I, too, am a druid, my friend, and I can assure you that we mean neither you nor your beautiful forest any harm."

"Well met," Ethen said after he had heard everything NeShae said. Then he continued, "But I have one question for you. Since you are the only one of the Power here, where did you learn of your gifts?"

NeShae didn't hesitate a moment before saying, "I guess I was born with them. However, I didn't know it until lately. You see, a friend helped me discover them, a friend named Merquilla."

"Merquilla?" Ethen asked curiously. "Merquilla the Sage?"

"Why, yes," NeShae said, shocked that he knew the name. "Do you know of her?"

"Everyone knows of Merquilla; she is a wise friend," Ethen answered her sincerely. "But how can I be sure that you are telling me the truth?"

NeShae started to think of something that could prove she knew Merquilla, but couldn't come up with anything until Alex said, "Show them the book she gave you."

NeShae understood and searched for the book that was hidden in the supplies in her backpack. After a moment, she pulled out a large, brown, leather-bound book with a silver lock on the front of it. She withdrew the key from within her robe and unlocked it. Then she handed the book to Ethen and watched as he opened the cover and read the words that Merquilla had written on the very first page: "NeShae, may this book help keep you from evil. Love, Merquilla." Ethen immediately looked to NeShae in an apologetic way as he continued, "My young travelers, I am so sorry. It's just that we must be careful around these parts as to who we let into our forest and our home. I do hope you will forgive us?"

Alex was the first to reply as he stepped forward and said, "Of course, we would have done the same thing in your position."

"Then will you join us in a feast to honor one with such great powers as to interest Merquilla?" Ethen asked as all three of the companions looked at each other in both shock and amazement.

"I think you must be mistaken," NeShae answered the old druid, "for I do not hold the powers you talk of. I can perform a few simple tricks, and can call upon a few stronger powers for a short time, but I am by no means a wielder of great powers."

"But my dear," Ethen said slowly after a short pause. "If Merquilla trained you, then believe me when I say that you have great powers, for the last druid she trained was the great Jonathon of Archwood, one of the most powerful druids known." He waited for a while before he said, "And that was over one hundred winters ago."

NeShae couldn't stop her mouth from dropping open after Ethen's last statement. "One hundred years?" she asked, bewildered. "But Merquilla looks so young!"

"Yes, my dear," Ethen answered her in the calm voice he had been using the entire time. "When a person lets herself become one with nature, beautiful things happen.   Just imagine how old I could be!" Ethen ended as he burst out into childish laughter, and soon the other druids joined him. Before long the whole forest was swarming with warmth, laughter, and joy.

Alex and Matthew both found this situation a little hard to comprehend, but they, too, joined in the laughter and watched as some of the men began carrying food to them from some unknown source—all kinds of food, all of which looked delicious and very edible. The food kept coming, and soon there were platters of it lying on every nearby stump and log. Then came the strong voice of Ethen once again, saying excitedly, "Let us feast well tonight!"

Matthew was the first to reach the food as he very willingly devoured everything that was within an arm's distance from him. Alex was a little more cautious though, and leaned closer to whisper to NeShae as the noises of singing and dancing became louder. "What do you think of all this?" he asked her quietly.

"I'm not really sure," NeShae told him, "but I do think they're sincere. Maybe they can even help us find some horses."

"Perhaps," Alex said, still deep in thought about what was happening. "Why don't we talk to Ethen right now?"

"Okay, if you want to," she answered him as she started walking over to where the druid was sitting, enjoying some food. NeShae approached Ethen and politely asked, "Would it be all right if we spoke to you in private?"

"Of course, of course, come with me," he answered as he got up and started into the forest. Alex looked over to Matthew to tell him what was happening, but decided not to when he noticed the size of the plate that the young boy was eating from. The prince quickly turned around and followed both NeShae and Ethen into the woods. Before long, they came to a small stream which neither Alex nor NeShae had even noticed before. They stopped there and waited for Ethen to say something. After a short wait, he did.

"What did you want to speak to me about, my children?" he asked them.

"Well, sir," Alex answered him, "we are in quite a hurry, and we were wondering if you knew of any way in which we could find some horses to speed our travels."

"Horses?" Ethen asked him, in what sounded like an almost disgusted voice. "Why would you travel by horse when such better means are available?"

"What do you mean?" NeShae asked him, puzzled by his last statement.

"Why go by land when you can fly?"

"Fly?" Alex asked in a bewildered tone. "But we do not have the means nor the magic to fly."

"Ah, but I do," the old man told them with a small smile as the twinkle in his eyes became even brighter.

"But in what manner could you make us fly?" NeShae asked.

"In a very natural one, I assure you," Ethen said to NeShae. Then he looked to her as he said, "My dear, you know that druids are very close to the animals, so why not ask them for a favor?"

"An animal?" Alex questioned loudly. "You want us to ride in the air on an animal? One we've never seen before? Are you crazy?"

"Alex," NeShae whispered to him in a tone that was meant to quiet the prince.

Alex didn't even look to NeShae, but instead continued to talk to Ethen. "How can we be sure that these animals would obey us, and not eat us for lunch?"

Ethen spoke, "Because we can communicate very well

with the animals, as I am sure NeShae knows, and I promise you that they will carry out anything we ask of them, without question or disobedience."

"Fly," Alex mumbled to himself, then looked to NeShae and said, "What do you think of this?"

"I think we can gain a lot of ground," she answered him. "And besides, I think I can maybe even communicate with the animal myself."

"Great," Alex said with a sigh, "We're going to put our lives in the hands of an animal that doesn't know us, and a practicing druid. Sounds fool-proof to me," he finished as he let out an unstoppable chuckle and shook his head.

NeShae smiled at him as she asked Ethen, "When can we leave?"

"When would you like to?" Ethen asked.

"As soon as we possibly can," Alex answered him.

Ethen slowly looked to the sky as he touched the medallion that hung loosely from his neck. He raised one hand, but left the other holding the round pendant around his neck. He started to clearly chant four words over and over again, and continued to watch the sky. NeShae and Alex were also watching, wondering what strange creature or creatures would appear. NeShae stood still, interested in seeing the animal that they were about to befriend. Alex, on the other hand, appeared to be a little more nervous, as he paced back and forth, never removing his eyes from the night above him. Soon they came. At first they appeared to be nothing but tiny birds, no bigger than squirrels. Before long they grew, and NeShae and Alex realized what they were looking at. The enormous birds landed; there were three of them.

Alex's mouth hung open as he gawked at their beauty and size. "They're eagles!" he said in amazement.

"That they are," Ethen whispered as he too wondered at their incredible beauty. NeShae walked slowly over to one of the large, peaceful-looking eagles, and gently touched her hand to the side of its head. The eagle returned her action as he rubbed his soft head against her cheek.

"Will they be able to carry us?" Alex asked as he turned again to face Ethen.

"Indeed, it will be no problem, they are very strong birds," Ethen answered him without a doubt. All of a sudden, the party heard a voice from behind the trees in the distance shout something.

"I think it was over here," came the voice of their friend and companion, Matthew, as he burst through the forest with his sword readied. He stopped in his tracks as he peered at the sight in front of him. As he was gawking, some of the other members of the druid clan came rushing out also, not knowing what to expect.

"What in the…where have you been?" Matthew asked them, still in bewilderment. "We saw these creatures fly over here, and we thought you might be in trouble. I guess we were wrong."

"Matthew," Alex started, "I'd like you to meet three beautiful flying friends of ours. They're going to be our transportation." Alex watched and laughed as his young companion's face grew very pale.

"My lord, the messenger has arrived," came the weary voice of the guard.

"Well, what are you waiting for?" the mage shouted. "Send him in immediately!"

"Yes, my lord."

Within a few moments, Galdon saw the young messenger whom he had sent to deliver the letter to the kingdom of Terrigrin. The boy hardly got in the door before Galdon started demanding answers from him.

"So, how did everything go?" he asked, in an unusually calm voice.

"Very well, my lord," the boy answered.

Galdon looked at him, expecting a little more of an answer, before he said sarcastically, "Do you think you could expand on that a little?"

"The queen said she would do anything to get her husband

back," the boy continued, somewhat frightened by the mage's hostile behavior. "She seemed really upset, and kept mentioning something about her son also being missing. I told her what you said, that you would even bring the king right to the castle if the money were ready."

"Very good boy, you have done well," Galdon told him. "Now get out of my sight."

"But my lord," the messenger said quietly after a short hesitation, "you promised me ten silver pieces if I did what you said."

"Yes I did, didn't I?" Galdon continued as he slowly made his way over to where the boy was standing. Each evil step brought him closer to where the young messenger's pounding heart and sweating palms where waiting. "But now I'm going to give you an even better deal. I'll let you keep your life for a measly ten silver pieces. Deal?"

"Yes…yes, my lord," the boy said, and then dashed for the doorway and out of the room. Galdon didn't waste any time before he stormed out of the room he was in and down the stairs to where the commander of his forces awaited him.

The man looked at Galdon with a smile. Galdon returned his look of satisfaction as he said, "We move in the morning. We'll get the army close enough to the kingdom of Terrigrin so that when our precious Kingy gives us the perfect chance to attack, they'll be ready; So go get them ready, we move at dawn."

"Alex, I'd like to laugh right along with you, but I don't find this situation very funny," Matthew told him in a very concerned voice, as the prince watched him with a smile on his face. "This isn't funny," he said again, trying to contain the grin that was trying so desperately to form on his face. "We could fall off of those…those things. Then what? Well, since none of us have any wings, it wouldn't be a pretty sight, now, would it? I mean it, Alex, I don't want to put my life in the hands, uh…claws, of anyone or anything else."

The prince looked sympathetically to Matthew, and then

walked over to his young companion and put a comforting arm around him as he said, "Matthew, I'd like to tell you that we had many other options, and that we could pass up this opportunity, but I can't. Just think of how much ground we can gain by taking flight! We've come this far, and I'm sorry, but we are going to be sitting on the backs of those eagles riding through the sky as soon as possible."

"You're right," Matthew said slowly with his eyes searching the ground. "It was selfish of me to disagree like that. I'm sorry."

"That's all right; you were only speaking your feelings," Alex said. "So are we ready to fly, or what?" Alex looked to NeShae, who was still caressing one of the eagle's heads. She looked at him with a large smile that told him of her approval to leave as soon as possible. He then looked back to Matthew, who gave him an uneasy grin. Finally he looked to Ethen, wondering what the old man would have to say. Ethen walked quietly up to Alex as eyes from all over the forest watched silently. When he reached the prince, he lifted his right arm and placed it on Alex's left shoulder.

"Good luck, my courageous friends," he started, "and may the winds always bring fine weather to you." Alex placed his right hand over the old druid's and nodded his head.

"Thank you, sir, for all you have done," Alex said sincerely.

NeShae broke the near-silent atmosphere with the words, "Well, boys, if we're going to fly, then let's get on with it." The other two understood completely, and they both hesitantly made their way over to the two vacant eagles, who were waiting with their heads down.

Matthew looked to Alex just before he climbed onto the large bird's back and choked out the words, "Alex, are you sure you want to do this?"

"Just get on," Alex laughed as he positioned himself on the back of his mount. Matthew closed his eyes, made a horrible face, and jumped onto the back of the waiting creature. The three companions waved to the druids who were standing in the forest, watching the three strangers who had only appeared a few hours before fly away. When Matthew opened his eyes again, they were in the air. NeShae took the lead, as it appeared to both Alex and Matthew that she shared something with her mount, almost as if she could understand it. They climbed higher until they were way above the treetops and they could hardly make out the shapes of the druids anymore. Matthew held onto his mount for dear life, while Alex and NeShae simply relaxed and enjoyed the beautiful scenery that was in front of them. The moon was nearly full and lit up the night sky like a candle, sending glistening beams off of every available object. The air was cool and almost magical, like a place that the party would like to enjoy forever. It felt as if they belonged there, and even Matthew got that feeling after he loosened his grip on his eagle's neck. The constant flapping of wings combined with the silence of the night almost put the party to sleep. It almost made them forget why they were there.

"They are ready, my lord," the commander answered as he entered Galdon's chambers.

"All of them?" the mage asked.

"Yes."

"What is their count?" Galdon asked.

"Around two hundred, my lord, including the wolves," the commander answered. "Is there anything else?"

"Yes," Galdon snapped, "I want you to tell them that we're moving out, right now."

"But my lord, dawn is hours away," the man responded.

Galdon gave the commander a look that told him to either obey or die, and so the commander went to relay the message to the army. As soon as he left, Galdon walked across the hall and into the large, finely made throne room where the king was waiting. "It has finally come," he began as he stared coldly into Dlemar's empty eyes. "Our time is here."

Dlemar didn't blink, but instead looked to the mage and said, without one hint of emotion, "Then let us begin."

"Look, to the left," Matthew said as he pointed, "That must be Tenlarick." The three of them could clearly make out the bright lights of the city below them.

"I think you're right," NeShae answered, turning to him.

"I think we can just keep going straight, then," Alex spoke. "Aren't those the Blue Mountains way off in the distance?"

"It looks like it," NeShae said, "but they still look like they're a long way away." The companions continued through the peaceful quietness of the night for a few hours before they noticed another small city, this time to the right, far below them.

"It must be Danden," Alex said to his other two friends. "Remember what Merquilla said about us being able to rest there?"

"Yes," NeShae answered him, "but she didn't know that we were going to be riding on the backs of eagles over the city, either."

Matthew spoke up, "Maybe we should just stop in for a few minutes to see what the place is like."

"I agree," Alex said, looking to NeShae for her opinion.

"Sure, why not?" she answered his look.

"Great," Alex continued. "Now, how do we get these things to take us down?"

"Leave that up to me," NeShae said with a laugh as she touched her hand softly on the back of her eagle's head. She slowly closed her eyes, and Alex and Matthew watched as she sat motionless on her mount for a few minutes. Finally, without any warning, the three creatures started descending in a circular fashion toward the city.

"I want you to take the main army with you," Galdon told the commander standing in front of him. "I'll be close behind with the king and a few guards, understand?"

"Yes, my lord," the commander answered obediently.

"And don't do anything stupid," Galdon continued. "I want you to stay low, and don't let them go running wild, or you'll have me to answer to. Now go. I'll be right behind you."

The man turned and exited the room as Galdon told him to. Then Galdon entered the throne room again and saw his prize sitting there, waiting for him. The king was ready.

"But what about the birds?" Matthew asked as they jumped from the backs of the eagles and onto the ground.

"I've told them to wait here until we get back," NeShae said as she stroked the head of one of them.

"But is it safe?" Matthew asked again as he looked around. They were just outside Danden, and they had managed to land in a fairly thick clump of trees.

"I'm sure they'll be fine," Alex answered and then started walking out of the woods and toward the main entrance to the city. They were greeted at the gate by a single guard who looked like he was only a young boy.

"What's your business in Danden?" he asked, obviously trying to deepen his voice.

Alex and NeShae tried to keep from laughing as the prince said, "We would like some food, for we have journeyed far."

"That will be five silver pieces each," the guard said slowly.

"Five silver pieces?" Alex asked, shocked at the price.

"Okay, two," the boy bargained.

Alex looked to NeShae, who was nodding her head as if she wanted him to pay the young lad, so he did. Then the three of them walked into the city of Danden together. They made their way down the main street of the small bustling community and were quite surprised at how lively it was, even in the middle of the night. Most of the stores were closed, except for a few small taverns which were dotted throughout the town. Next to one of these they noticed a sign which read The Swirling Winds Tavern.

"That must be the place," Alex said as they started walking toward it. Just as they were about to enter the building, Matthew tugged on Alex's shoulder and said something.

"What?" Alex asked him as he turned around to face Matthew.

"Look," Matthew said excitedly as he pointed to the disgusting form of a figure that was familiar to all of them as an orc. The creature was pushing one of the city guards around, and had just drawn its sword. The image of the sword shocked the party and made NeShae's heart almost leap from her body. It was black and had a large letter G carved on its blade, the exact description of the weapon she was looking for.

A TOUGH DECISION

NeShae looked to Alex, not quite knowing what to do next, and said, "Well, let's do something!"

Alex was still watching the large vile creature push the much smaller guard around. A crowd was starting to form, and Alex wondered if any more guards would come to help. By the size of the small town, however, he doubted it. After a few moments, he looked to NeShae and answered, "Let's go get him." Then he looked to Matthew and continued, "You sneak around behind him and wait, just in case we run into trouble, okay?"

"Sure," Matthew answered as he started off, making his way toward the orc while trying to stay hidden.

Alex gave a final look to NeShae before he grabbed his sword and started running toward the orc. The guard was the first to notice the prince, as his eyes gawked at the curious stranger was running toward them. The orc turned to see what the guard was looking at just in time to deflect an almost-fatal blow aimed at his neck. The large creature threw the young guard to the side and directed all of his attention at Alex. The weapon he held was entirely black and radiated an obvious evilness. The second blow was from the orc, and it almost knocked Alex to the ground as he parried it. Alex quickly regained his composure and made a counter that nearly shaved the disgusting orc's foul flesh. By this time, Matthew was in position to strike, waiting patiently for the right moment to leap from the shadows and plant his dagger deep into the orc's hide. The two continued to exchange blows, and finally the orc's back was facing Matthew. He made his move. The blade of his dagger sunk deep into the skin of the wretched monster, but Matthew remained alert and ducked just in time to save himself from a retaliating swing. Alex saw his chance, and without hesitation thrust his weapon into the side of the screaming orc. Slowly, the orc fell to its knees, and then went still as the large black weapon it was holding fell to the ground. NeShae came rushing to Alex and Matthew as soon as she saw that they had attained victory. Alex was standing over the orc's dead body, telling the new-formed crowd of people around them that everything was okay and that they could leave. Matthew just stood there, staring at the creature's motionless figure, holding his bloody dagger. Alex took a few steps over to Matthew and put a reassuring hand on his shoulder as he whispered, "It's all right."

Matthew's eyes made their way up to Alex's as he answered with a smile, "Yeah, I know."

Alex bent down and reached for the weapon that was resting on the ground. He picked it up, walked over to NeShae, and placed it in her hands. "Here, now take this back to your brother. If you hurry, there will still be enough time to save him."

NeShae's face turned a deep red after the prince's words, not from embarrassment or heat, but from anger. "How dare you tell me to leave you! I thought we were all in this together, but maybe I was wrong." Then she turned and started walking away. Alex knew that she had misunderstood him, so he quickly caught up to try to reason with NeShae's stubborn side.

"NeShae, I did not mean it that way," the prince started. "I simply meant that I would like something good to come out of this horrible situation, and if that means your brother being saved, then I want you to do it. I don't want you to leave, but you must remember why you are even here. Please, don't be angry, but take the weapon to your brother. Matthew can accompany you."

Matthew's face lit up with dispute, but he knew that if that was what Alex wanted him to do, he would do it. "But Alex, we can't leave you. We've been through so much together, we just can't."

"You have to; don't you understand?" Alex continued. "If we all get killed trying to save my father, then what about NeShae's brother? Besides, I can travel faster alone, so please do as I say." Alex turned his gaze toward the horizon as he waited for a response.

"If that's what you want," NeShae answered. "Come on, Matthew, we've got a long road ahead of us."

Alex looked back to them with an approving smile and said, "Everything will be fine." Then he walked over to NeShae, lifted her hand, and kissed it. "You are more of a princess than anyone I have ever known, and someday I will prove it to you." He kissed her teary face gently, and then walked over to Matthew. The prince grabbed Matthew's hand and shook it. "Matthew, you are no longer a young boy; you have proven yourself. I would be proud to fight next to you anytime. Now you take good care of NeShae, or you'll have me to answer to, understand?" Matthew nodded his head and smiled. Alex didn't say another word, but instead turned and started walking toward what appeared to be a stable.

NeShae turned to Matthew, a small grin on her face, and said, "Does he really think he can get rid of us that easily?"

Matthew knew she was up to something but just shook his head and laughed.

The darkness of the still night was mitigated on by many small campfires spread in different patterns. There were small tents placed here and there around Galdon's encampment, waiting for dawn and another day of travel. This was their second day of travel, and they were making fairly good time, for they were already out of the Blue Mountains. Galdon sat in his tent, which was clearly the largest and most decorative of the bunch, with his willing prisoner and his commander of the army.

"How far is it before we reach Danden?" Galdon asked without even looking at the commander.

"We should reach it tomorrow by dusk, my lord."

"Good, but make sure no one escapes. I don't want anyone to know what is happening."

"Yes, my lord. I have only one question. Why are we taking over such a small town that is so far from Terrigrin?"

"You've seen how hungry the army is for blood, Commander," Galdon answered. "It's better to satisfy that need now than to wait until they have a chance to ruin my plans."

"Yes, my lord," the commander responded, and exited his master's tent.

"Well, Kingy, what do you think of my plans now?" Galdon asked in a sneering voice.

"They are perfect, my lord," was the king's only reply.

NeShae and Matthew made their way to where they had left their large winged friends. Matthew was still curious as to what NeShae was planning to do, but he asked no questions. He watched as she took a small piece of parchment from her backpack and scribbled something on it. Then she took the black weapon that she was holding and tied it and the parchment to the back of one of the eagles. She whispered something to one of the eagles and gently stroked its head. Within seconds the large birds had taken flight, without passengers, in the same direction from which they had come. NeShae looked to Matthew, who was simply shaking his head.

"What?" she asked him as she tried to conceal the smile that was forming on her face.

"Nothing," Matthew smirked. "Nothing at all."

"Good, then let's get back to business, okay?"

Matthew nodded in compliance, and they started back to the city to find Alex.

"I need a good strong horse," Alex told the man standing behind the bar of the Swirling Winds Tavern. The man looked at him questioningly until Alex added, "Merquilla sent me."

"I've got lot's of 'em," the middle-aged man responded positively. "Come with me." The man exited the tavern through a rear doorway and walked to a well-concealed stable in the back. "Go ahead, take your pick."

Alex carefully examined each of the ten or so horses that were in front of him until he found what he thought was the perfect one. "I'll take that one," he responded as he pointed to an entirely white mount.

"Oh, she's a beaut," the man answered Alex as he walked over and started caressing the horse. "Her name's Dee, and she can run like the wind."

"How much?" Alex asked without hesitation.

"Not a thing," came the reply from the man. "A favor for Merquilla is payment enough."

"Thank you very kindly, sir," Alex replied as he walked over to his new steed. "Your compassion is appreciated."

The man smiled as Alex led his new companion from the stables. He exited and was again in the center of the small town of Danden. Just as he was starting toward the gate to leave, he heard the familiar voice of NeShae call his name. Without even turning around, he dropped his head, waiting to hear why they weren't gone yet.

As soon as they were close enough, he turned around quickly and snapped, "What are you doing here? I told you to take that weapon back to your brother. That doesn't mean follow me around."

"Don't worry," NeShae answered him calmly. "Everything is under control. I sent the weapon back with the eagles."

"Everything is under control?" Alex continued in a harsh tone. "Everything would be under control if you would have done as I asked. This isn't a game, NeShae! We could die. Now please, I'll get you some horses and you can go back while you still can. I don't want to feel guilty because you got hurt trying to help me with my problems. So here's some money, now…"

"Well, you spoiled little brat," NeShae said in a disgusted tone, surprising both Alex and Matthew. "Do you actually think that we should just leave you here alone to die? We all know that our chances of success are much greater if we are together, so don't you dare tell me what I can and can't do. We're not in your kingdom anymore, and I can do as I please, so I'm going with you whether you like it or not."

"Me, too," Matthew agreed.

Alex looked to the ground, trying to fight the smile that was forming on his face, and said only one thing, "Then let's get you some horses."

They went back to where Alex had gotten his horse, and in less than an hour, the three of them were leaving the city of Danden,together.

The three companions traveled silently in the darkness of the early morning, making their way north toward the mountains that were looming in the far distance. Each of their heads was filled with different thoughts as they continued on, but they were all thinking of what was waiting for them in the mountains that seemed to get closer with each passing second. Alex looked to NeShae from time to time, making sure that she was safe, and every time he did, he got the same, girlish grin from her, which meant that she was just fine.

It seemed like forever before the sun finally started to show on the eastern horizon. It was still too dark to make out exactly where they were, though. It was then that Matthew noticed a small light in the distance. It wasn't like a house light, but a smaller one, almost like a campfire. As he looked carefully around, he noticed that there were more of these small lights, dozens of them. He stopped abruptly as he told Alex of his observation and pointed out the lights in the distance.

"Do you really think they're lights?" NeShae asked curiously. "I mean, they could be fireflies or something."

"No," Alex answered as he stared at the mysterious lights. "Matthew is right. They almost look like campfires."

"Well," Matthew asked after a small hesitation, "What should we do?"

Alex continued to stare at the lights as he contemplated their next move. "One of us should check it out."

"Why don't we all go?" NeShae asked.

"Because there's a greater chance of us being spotted if we all go," Alex answered her.

"Then I'll go," Matthew told them.

"Are you sure?" the prince asked.

"Yes."

"Okay, but be careful; you haven't much time before the sun comes up. Just remember to stay low, and don't do anything stupid. We just want to know what's going on over there," Alex told him.

"Don't worry," Matthew said with a grin. "Remember, I've lived on the streets my whole life. This should be easy."

"Just be careful," NeShae said with a motherly look.

"I will," he said, and rode off into the night.

Matthew quietly directed his horse toward the faint lights that he saw in front of him. As he slowly made his way closer, he realized that if he were going to be successful, he would have to continue on foot, for his horse was making more noise than he wanted. So after a few more yards, Matthew quietly dismounted and tied his animal companion to one of the nearby trees. From there he continued on foot. The lights were getting closer quite rapidly, as was the approaching dawn, and Matthew traveled as fast as he dared without making too much noise. He knew that he didn't have much time before the light broke, and then he would be visible. It wasn't long before he could make out what the source of the lights were. There were many small campfires spread out in front of him, and it appeared that there were also a number of tents scattered about. With the help of the slowly forming dawn, he could see that there were dozens of tents set up around the area of the campfires. He could barely make out the large, humanoid forms that were pacing around this encampment, but he knew that they were there, and there were a lot of them. He carefully searched every single tent, trying to look for anything that might give him a clue as to what he was looking at. One by one, however, they all proved to be almost the same in appearance—except for one. It was set in the very middle of the camp, and was much larger than the others. It also had two guards posted outside of the entrance.

Matthew sat down for a moment, trying to think of what to do next. He looked back in the direction of Alex and NeShae, but he was too far away from them to see the companions that he now wished were by his side. He looked to the slowly forming light of the morning sun, and finally to the large tent in the middle of the camp. Then he stood up and quickly, but quietly, started toward the tent. Because of the trees that dotted the terrain, Matthew was easily able to get right up close to the camp without being noticed. In front of him and only a few yards away was a large creature with grayish skin and sharp teeth that managed to stick out of its pig-like snout. Its ears were pointed, and it was standing there with a battle ax. Matthew stood still for a moment, trying to decide what to do next. The horizon was getting lighter with every breath he took, and he knew he had to do something quickly. He slowly took one of the daggers from his black leather boot, raised it, and gave a silent prayer. Then he released it into the air. It sailed straight and silent, and struck the creature in the throat. Matthew didn't even crack a smile, but instead looked around and darted behind one of the tents that were in front of him. He could now see the large tent, for it was right in front of him. He was just about to make a break for the other side when he saw something exit the doorway between the two guards. It was a human, dressed in a long robe. Behind him came another human, this one wearing a crown, and dressed much fancier than the first. Matthew watched their actions carefully as the first man walked over to one of the guards.

He could only hear parts of the conversation, and the man saying, "Let the men…it's only a small town…but be quick."

Matthew couldn't hear any more of the conversation, so he turned his attention to the man with the crown on his head. He was dressed in very elegant clothes, and Matthew knew that he must be a very high-class individual. Matthew continued to watch him, looking for any signs of his role in this strange scenario. The crowned man didn't even show any hint of emotion, but instead stood still, with only a blank look on his face. It was starting to get light enough to see now, and Matthew knew that he would have to end his spying. He carefully turned his back and started off. It was then that he heard the first man's voice give an order: "Dlemar, let's go; we've got lands to conquer."

Matthew froze. His head started spinning with disbelief. "Dlemar!" he whispered to himself as he fought to contain the excitement that was ready to burst from within him. "Alex's father!" he said just loud enough for himself to hear. Matthew turned and hastily took off in the same direction from which he had come. He didn't want to alert anyone to his unwanted presence, but Matthew was excited. He had to get back to tell Alex the good news. His pace grew faster and soon he was out of the camp. Matthew found his horse waiting patiently in the same place that he had left him. Matthew jumped on and directed his animal friend in Alex and NeShae's direction. It wasn't long before he arrived, with an excited face and a huge smile. Alex and NeShae immediately came to him.

"What took you so long?" Alex asked in a worried tone. "Is anyone following you?" he continued as he searched the terrain for any sign of movement.

"No," Matthew said, still grinning widely. "But I've got some great news. I saw…"

"Why don't you get something to eat first?" NeShae interrupted him. "You must be quite hungry."

"I'm not hungry! I have some news—"

"Well, what is it?" Alex asked.

"I'd tell you if you'd both stop interrupting me," he said in a joking voice. Then Matthew calmed down and looked into Alex's eyes. "I saw your father."

"What!" Alex said as his heart almost leapt into his throat.

"I saw your father!" Matthew continued, now laughing ecstatically. "He was in the camp, with a crown on his head. There was another man with him, and he said something about a town, and to be quick because the men deserve it, and…"

"Slow down," NeShae said as she put a hand on Matthew's shoulder. "Now tell us what happened from the beginning." So all three of the companions sat down while Matthew told his story in its entirety. When Matthew was done, the two friends both looked to Alex for their next move. Matthew stood still for what seemed like an eternity to the other two friends.

Without warning, he finally said, "Then we're going to have to go get him." Even though NeShae and Matthew both knew that was coming, they were still were a little surprised after hearing it. After all, Matthew had said that there was an army camped there! Alex continued after a short hesitation, "We'll make our move tonight, when it's dark. We'll be in and out of the camp with my father before they can even realize he's gone. So we have to stay out of sight until then. Which way did you say they were headed, Matthew?"

"I'm not sure. I think they were coming from the north, though."

"From the north, huh?" Alex thought out loud. "Then they should be passing through Danden in a few hours. If we…" Alex stopped suddenly and jerked his head to Matthew. "What did you say you heard about the town?"

"Well, I couldn't make out much, except for something

about a town, and the men deserving such a plunder."

"Danden!" Alex exclaimed as he started frantically searching for the rest of his somewhat scattered belongings.

NeShae searched Alex's face for some sign of what he was thinking and finally asked, "What is it? What's wrong, Alex?"

"Maybe nothing," Alex continued as he picked up his finely made bow and placed it on his shoulder. "But what if this army is headed for Danden for their plunder? I mean, it makes sense, because it's the closest town for miles."

"Well, we have to do something," NeShae added as she, too, began picking up the few items that were still scattered about on the ground.

"We have to get to Danden and warn them about what's happening," Alex replied as he walked over to his horse and began loading his mount with gear. Both Matthew and NeShae did the same, and within minutes they were all headed in the same direction from which they had come only a day earlier. They rode hard, stopping for neither food nor rest, the entire time watching their backs, searching for any sign of the army behind them. Because of their steady riding, the party reached the city of Danden shortly after sunset and rode up to the gates together.

Alex saw the same guard that they had encountered the first time they had entered the city, a few days earlier. Not wanting to waste any time, the prince hopped off his horse and spoke. "I need to see whoever is in charge of your city."

"In charge?" the young guard asked curiously as his eyes searched Alex, looking for some explanation.

"Yes—your mayor, chief, leader, king you know, the person in charge."

"Well, tonight I'm in charge," the boy answered proudly as he slightly pushed out his scrawny chest.

"I'm serious," Alex continued, now getting quite angry with the young boy's sarcasm.

"So am I," he answered.

"You mean to tell me that you, a young guard boy, has the responsibility of making decisions which may affect the entire city?" Alex questioned him in a harsh voice.

"Yes; it's the guard's privilege," he answered with an honest face.

"The guard's privilege," Alex mumbled as he looked to NeShae and Matthew and shook his head. "So how many of you guards are there?"

"Three."

"Three!" Alex shouted unbelievingly. "But—but you're a city! You have to have more than three guards!"

"Not really," the boy answered Alex. "You see, we haven't had any major enemies for over a hundred years, so we don't have much need for an army."

"Well, what about a leader?"

"Oh, we have a leader, but right now he's in Donaville on business."

"And so you're the next in command," Alex said, finishing the boy's train of thought.

"Yup. It's always been that way. It's not like we ever have to make any decisions or anything. Besides, we aren't really a city. More like a large village," he finished with a small chuckle.

"Well, my young friend, you're about to rewrite history as the first guard to ever make a major decision," Alex told the boy.

"What are you talking about?" the guard asked Alex, again looking quite suspicious.

Matthew explained what he had seen and heard. The guard simply listened, not quite knowing whether to believe these strangers or not. Finally, Matthew finished his story and the three companions looked to the young guard, waiting for his reaction. His face was blank, and his eyes didn't blink for minutes. Alex, afraid that the boy was going to pass out, said something. "We need you to alert the city and tell them what is happening. It has to be done quickly, before the army arrives."

The guard didn't respond, but just stood there, staring at the ground. Finally he said, "But I wouldn't know what to say."

Alex looked to his two friends and rolled his eyes. Then he looked back to the boy and said, "Then let me say it. All you have to do is give me permission."

The guard looked to each of the three companions' faces, searching for any solution that they might have to the problem. He waited for what seemed like forever to Alex, and finally looked at the prince and said, "Okay, I'm giving you permission."

Alex's face relaxed and broke into a smile as he spoke, "Then let's get going."

Ptilon the falcon circled the cool air of the dark night, searching for any news that he could bring his master, Artimus. He could sense trouble, but he couldn't tell what it was. He lifted his head and drifted effortlessly into the night.

A LEADER IS BORN

"We need to call a town meeting," Alex told the guard.

"A town meeting?" the young boy responded. "In the middle of the night?"

"Yes," Alex answered him in a tone that left no room for argument.

"Okay, okay. I'll go ring the bell." The three friends watched as the boy walked over to a small, two-story tower which was standing very near them. He opened the only entrance to the small square building, walked in, and pulled a thick cord that hung down from above. They heard the sound of a loud echoing bell which rang once, then twice, then three times. The guard exited the tower, shut the door, and then walked back to where Alex, NeShae, and Matthew were waiting.

"They should all be here soon," he said, directing his comment at Alex.

"Good," Alex replied and waited. Within minutes people started showing up, coming from all different directions. Men, women, children, and the elderly were all there. In a very short time, every single person in the small town was there, and they were all mumbling to each other about what was going on, looking to the young guard and strangers for answers.

Alex wasted no time. When he realized that everyone was there, he looked at NeShae, who gave him a reassuring wink and smile, and then he stepped forward. "Townsfolk of Danden, I come to you bearing news of great importance. I am Prince Alexander Denmoore of the kingdom of Terrigrin, and I am here on an urgent matter. Less than a day's travel from here is a large army that is planning to march through your city, stopping for nothing in its way." After this, there was a large amount of noise which came from the crowd—the noise of people talking about what was happening.

The voice of a middle-aged man came from the crowd, saying "You mean to tell us that after over a hundred years of peace, some army is going to come out of the middle of nowhere to take our town?" There were some shouts of disbelief from the crowd again as Alex tried to convince them.

"I know this may be hard to believe, my friends, but it is true," Alex continued. "We have seen this army and believe that they are headed here to take your city."

"What would they want with our city?" came a voice.

"We're not sure, but we do think that you are in grave danger if you aren't prepared."

The voice of a young woman spoke, "Prepared? Prepared for what? If there actually is an army marching toward us, do you think that we could stop them? Look at us, my prince; we are simple townsfolk, not soldiers."

"You are right—you are simple townsfolk," Alex began, "but you are also men and women with homes and children. By standing together, you have a chance against this foe. Would you rather run in fear, or stand and fight for the rights of your children to continue living peacefully in this town for years to come?"

"But why do you, the prince of Terrigrin, care what happens to a small village such as us?" shouted a man in the back.

Alex looked at the two hundred or so people that were standing in front of him, thinking of what he should say, when he finally answered. "Because my father, King Dlemar Denmoore, has been taken hostage by this army's leader for some unknown purpose, and I will do anything in my power to get him back." The whispers of the crowd grew with Alex's last statement, but quieted again when the prince spoke. "So, my friends, I am going to stand and defend your homes, whether it be alone or not. I am asking if you are going to stand beside me or leave. But let it be known that I would be honored to fight beside each and every one of you." Alex watched the crowd carefully, hoping that his speech had done the trick.

After a short hesitation, one man stepped forward and said, "I'm staying." Soon another did the same. And another. After a few short minutes, every last person had agreed to stay and fight for their homes.

After the new army had formed, one woman spoke up. "So now what?"

"We have to start preparing immediately," Alex answered her and the rest of the townspeople. "We can't wait until sunrise, for we have little time. What do you have for weapons?" Alex asked the young guard.

"We have some bows and swords, but that is it."

"Is there a weapon smith present?" Alex asked the entire crowd.

Immediately a short muscular man stepped forward and said, "That is my, my prince. How can I be of service?"

"I want you to bring all of your stored weapons out and set them here," Alex told him as he pointed to the ground in front of him. Then he looked back to the crowd again and asked, "How about a fletcher?" A thin young man stepped forward this time, and Alex addressed him. "I need every single arrow you can find or make. These fine people will help you," he finished, pointing to two men and two women in the front. They left at once, eager to do their jobs. "As for the rest of you, I need every weapon in this village, whether it be a club or a sword, brought here. We need every weapon we can find." The crowd slowly thinned, and Alex looked again to the young guard at his side. "What did you say your name was?"

"James," the boy answered.

"Well, James, does this town have any larger weapons, like a catapult or something?" Alex asked, hoping that the answer would be yes.

"Nope," James answered, almost ashamed. "Our only defense is our wall."

Alex turned his head to the fifteen-foot-high wall that surrounded the entire town, looking for any weaknesses that it held. Then he looked back to James and said, "Then we have to make one."

"Make one?" James exclaimed. "But I don't even know..."

"I know, but I do," Alex cut him off. "My father made very sure of that." Alex looked to NeShae as a small smile appeared on his face. Alex saw that the townsfolk had already started to bring their weapons, and the small pile was already starting to grow, as was a small crowd of people.

Alex stepped forward to address the small group that was waiting for another job. "You have done well in bringing these weapons," the prince started, "but I fear that we will need even more powerful devices. That is why we are going to build a catapult." The small group looked at each other in amazement and disbelief. "Do not fear," the prince continued, "for I know how to construct one, but I need all of your help. And I need it quickly." Alex looked around, noticing some small children playing not too far away. He whispered something to NeShae, and then went over to the group to begin construction on the catapult.

NeShae walked casually over to the ten or twelve children who were playing so innocently in front of her. They were playing a popular game with rocks, so NeShae bent down to talk with them. "What kind of a game are you playing?" she asked one of the older girls.

"Oh, nothing," the girl answered and continued to toss rocks near a large basket that was in the center of the circle of children.

"Well, I know of a very fun game, if you'd like to play," NeShae continued.

All of the children's ears perked up, almost as though they were dogs. One of the younger boys asked, "What kind of a game is it?"

"It's a game to see who can collect the most rocks in a basket," she answered them in a gentle voice.

"But what fun is that?" the young boy asked again.

"Because the winner gets this beautiful scarf," NeShae said as she pulled off one of the scarves that were wrapped around her neck. It was red and silky and it definitely caught the attention of some of the children. Unfortunately, it only caught the girls' attention.

"Yuk!" one of the boys yelled. "I'm not no girl. What would I do with a dumb old scarf?"

NeShae searched her head for an idea, then reached over to one of the patches that were hidden so well on her magical robe and pulled it off.

"If one of you boys win, then you can have this magical rope," NeShae told him, hoping it would do the trick. It did. NeShae didn't even have time to say another word, for every child there was gone, each with his or her own baskets, looking for every single rock that he or she could find. NeShae stood up, smiled, and walked back to where Matthew and James were standing.

"The sun will be up in a few hours," Matthew stated as he looked at the horizon. "What do you say we make a huge breakfast for everyone? You know, to raise morale and everything."

James agreed with the idea, and hastily went to one of the larger buildings aythe far end of the town. Matthew looked to NeShae and said, "I'll go help him with the food, okay?"

"Okay," she answered. "I'm going to go see how Alex is doing." So they parted, and Matthew went to help James with the food that was going to be used for breakfast. NeShae made her way over to where Alex and about ten others were constructing the catapult. She saw trees, rope, and pitch lying all around, and managed to catch Alex's figure cutting at one of the trees. She walked over to him and gently put her arms around his waist.

"And how is my prince?" she asked as she felt his muscles relax.

Alex turned around slowly and looked into the eyes that had given him so much comfort on this long journey. "I'm not sure, NeShae," he answered. "What am I doing? I've put these poor people in jeopardy. They could lose their homes, or even worse, their lives, and all because of my greed in wanting my father back."

"Don't be silly," NeShae told him as she gently rubbed his shoulders. "If you hadn't come here in the first place, the entire town would have been caught off guard, and they would have been destroyed without a fight. And they all know that. Alex, you have done nothing wrong, and you should be proud of your accomplishments. Few people in the realm could have done what you have. Remember that."

"But I could have never done it without you and Matthew. I owe you so much. I only hope that your brother has been saved by now, and that one good thing has come out of this."

"I'm sure he has," NeShae comforted him. "But for now, we have to worry about a very large obstacle that is marching our way, probably at this moment."

"At times, you have more strength than a thousand men, NeShae," the prince continued as he watched her face grow red. "Sometimes I think that you should have been the princess and I should have been the peasant."

"Now wouldn't that be a sight?" NeShae said as she laughed out loud.

"It is a sight that I would like to see," the prince said very seriously.

"I'm afraid that one is out of your power, my prince," she told him, chuckling again.

"But, my beautiful lady, it is not," Alex said as he took her hand in his. NeShae's face wore a puzzled look as she searched for an explanation to the prince's words. "What I am trying to say, or ask, is if, after all of this is over, you would be my wife."

NeShae's face softened as the tears began rolling down her face. She grabbed Alex and squeezed him tightly. "Oh, yes, Alex," she answered him as she sobbed in his ear. "I would love to."

They embraced for a moment, but then stopped as they heard the sound of applause behind them. They both looked over to where the sound was coming from, and saw that a small crowd had formed. Then they realized that they had been talking loud enough the entire time that everyone could hear them. They both burst into laughter and hugged again. Almost the entire crowd had smiles on their faces and tears in their eyes as they watched this touching event. Finally, Alex turned to them and spoke. "All right, all right, it's time to get back to work." He turned and gave NeShae a kiss on the cheek and walked back to where he had been before. NeShae made her way to where Matthew and James had already begun piling eggs, ham, and bread. They were in the very center of the village, an open area, with a large fire in the center. NeShae helped some of the women begin making breakfast over the open flames as Matthew and James started pulling tables from various buildings outside. Then Matthew noticed Alex walking toward them, so they stopped to talk for a moment.

"The catapult is going to take longer than I thought," Alex started. "But I've got some of the women boiling hot oil on top of the wall, in case the trees try to climb it. NeShae has some of the children collecting rocks to use for the catapult, in slings, for dumping over the wall, or whatever else we need them for. We have every weapon in the village, and a lot of the men are helping make arrows, because I think we have enough bows for everyone. I have enough pitch and oil for the catapult missiles, so that job is finished. But there are still quite a few men without jobs, so after breakfast I want you to take as many as you can outside, James. I need you to dig trenches around the entire wall, about three or four feet deep, and the same distance wide. Then cover them with twigs and branches and stuff. We're going to need everything we can get to slow them down. Hopefully NeShae can help out a little with her powers. Now, I know that everyone will want to take a long break for breakfast, but don't let them. Give them food and get them back to work, okay? I'm giving that responsibility to you two."

"Okay," Matthew answered as James also nodded in response. "But what are you going to do?"

"The catapult has to get finished, and we have to make sure that everyone who has a bow knows how to fire it. I'm giving that job to you, Matthew. After breakfast, I want you to take the men and boys who are working with the arrows and make sure that they know what they're doing. Make sure they have plenty of arrows and know where to stand on the wall when it's time. When the men who will be digging are finished, make sure that they also know how to fire their bows, and give them positions on the wall. I want as many archers as we can possibly fit on that wall. We should be able to get at least one hundred of them up there with the amount of weapons we have. Any problems?"

"Nope," Matthew answered, as did James.

"Good," Alex said, and turned and walked away.

Not long after that, the sun was starting to poke its way over the horizon, and the women who were making breakfast had already begun serving it. The bell that rang signaled to everyone that it was time to stop working and time to begin eating. Within minutes, the entire town, except for Alex, was in the middle of the village, eating the wonderfully prepared food that was in front of them.

Alex set the tools that he was working with down for a moment, and climbed one of the ladders on the inside of the wall that led to the top of their primary defense. He searched the land for any sign of movement, but he could see none because of the few trees that dotted the landscape. He sat there for a moment, admiring the beauty of the land. The horizon was painted a faint red as the sun was just trying to make its way over the treetops. The sounds of the birds had started echoing throughout the land, and he watched above him as the clouds moved slowly by. Alex shook his head and smiled, and then climbed back down his ladder to continue his work.

"I'm sorry, folks," Matthew spoke loud enough for everyone to hear, "but we don't have any time to spare. As soon as you are done eating, we have to get back to work." He told everyone of their jobs, and watched as James led a small group of men outside with shovels to start work on the trench. Matthew, on the other hand, stayed inside and helped with the weapons. He noticed that almost all of the townspeople were quite proficient with the bow and arrow, which surprised him, but was also very relieving. After a few hours he had made sure that everyone had a bow and plenty of arrows, and knew his positions on the wall when it was time for battle. Matthew had just finished with the first group when James came back with a shovel over his shoulder.

"Did you finish the trench?" Matthew asked him as he got closer.

"Yup," James answered him as he stopped and leaned on the shovel.

"Good. I have to make sure that all of your men have weapons, and know how to use them." Matthew walked over to where the workers were standing and told them what their next task was. Then he led them over to where the extra weapons were sitting, and where there were still a few men and boys making arrows.

The sun had fully risen by now and Alex was pushing his workers harder than ever to finish the catapult that they were working on. He hadn't talked to NeShae since their last conversation, but he had seen her walk into one of the homes about an hour earlier. He had guessed that she was preparing whatever magical spells that she intended on using, but he wasn't sure. Hours passed and it was near the middle of the day before the prince finally let his workers take a break for lunch. The morale of the townspeople seemed fairly high, as everything seemed to be going as planned, and they seemed to enjoy the company and leadership of the prince and his friends. Alex continued to work on the catapult even after the men had gone to lunch. While he was working, Matthew approached him.

"How's everything going?" he asked the prince.

"Fine," Alex answered in a dull voice. "How about you?"

"Fine," Matthew answered. "Every man and boy who is old enough to fight has a weapon, knows how to use it, and knows exactly where to go when it's time. We even went through a couple of drills to make sure."

"What about the oil? And the rocks? Did the trench get finished?"

"Yes, yes, and yes," Matthew answered him with a chuckle. "There's nothing to worry about, Alex; everything is going great."

"Everything except for this catapult, that is," Alex answered him as he pounded on the unfinished machine.

"I'm sure you'll have it finished in no time," Matthew reassured him.

"I sure hope so. Oh, by the way, I want you to post a couple of lookouts on the wall. They shouldn't be here for at least a few more hours, but I want to be sure. If they see anything, have them give you a signal, and prepare everything as planned. It's very important, however, that the enemy thinks we have no clue as to what is happening, so make sure everyone knows that, okay?"

"Sure, I'll make sure that the men stay hidden until they're within range." Matthew turned to make his way back to where the townspeople were gathered when he heard Alex's voice.

"Matthew," the prince said softly, "thanks for everything. I owe you a lot, and when we finally make it out of this nightmare, I plan to repay you."

Matthew turned again to face the prince and stated, "Alex, you've already repaid me more than I could ever have asked.

It is me who owes you." Then he turned and walked off.

Another hour or two passed. Alex still had seen no sign of NeShae since early that morning, but he wasn't worried, for he knew that when the time came, he could depend on her. In the middle of his thoughts, he heard the sound of footsteps behind him. It was James, and he walked directly up to Alex and began to speak.

"The lookouts think that they see something, a long way off."

"How long before they get here?" Alex asked, not surprised at the news.

"Probably within an hour," James answered, waiting for a reply.

"If we could only get this catapult finished by then!" Alex shouted as he threw one of the tools against a wooden brace on the machine.

"Calm down, my lovely prince," a calm, beautiful voice said as both Alex and James turned their heads. They saw NeShae standing with her staff, watching Alex with a girlish smile. NeShae watched as Alex smiled the only smile that he had shown since the sun had risen. "Maybe I can help," she said as she walked over to the wooden contraption. The workers, Alex, and James all watched as she gently caressed the rough wood, searching the entire object with her eyes. She did this for a few minutes before finally stopping at one particular point. She slowly closed her eyes and chanted some very unfamiliar words. Right before everyone's eyes, the entire object, including those pieces not finished, starting bending, shaping, and fastening themselves together. Every unfinished article that was awaiting its purpose suddenly found itself a part of the large machine. No one could even speak as they watched this miraculous sight, wondering what was coming next. At last, NeShae stopped, put her hands on her hips, and turned to look at Alex, who was standing with his mouth wide open.

"Now, isn't that much easier?" she chuckled.

Alex simply shook his head as he looked at the newly

finished catapult in front of him and listened to the workers' excitement around him. "You're incredible," was all that he could manage to say before Matthew came running toward them.

"They're getting closer, and fast!" he exclaimed when he got close enough for them to understand.

"Okay, let's get the catapult ready to fire, and make sure everyone is in position, Matthew," the prince commanded.

"Is the catapult going to be able to fire over the wall?" James asked as the men started moving the wheeled machine.

"I sure hope so," the prince answered, not able to contain the smile that was forming on his face. Alex wasn't sure of the reason for his smile, whether it was because everything was going so smoothly or because he was excited, but he knew that it was there.

NeShae walked over to Alex's side and touched his hand. "Don't worry, Alex; you deserve this. Besides, I just might have a few more surprises up my sleeve."

Alex gave her a kiss on the lips, grabbed the bow from his shoulder and whispered, "I love you." NeShae's eyes lit up as she watched him walk over to the wall, where everyone was preparing for the battle that was soon to take place.

"I love you, too," she whispered.

The birds had received her call and had started on their way, eager to help this new friend that they had made. They soared through the air, wasting no time, for they knew the urgency of the call. They only hoped they could be there in time.

THE ROAD COMES TO AN END

Alex watched carefully as the mass of bodies grew closer, trying to see clearly through the few trees that scattered the landscape. He looked to his side, making sure that everything was ready. Every able man and boy who had a bow was on top of the wall, concealed by the stone parapet that was constructed atop the wall. Alex slowly looked again through the battlement that was right next to him, one of the many open areas used to fire through, placed systematically around the parapet. It seemed like time wasn't even moving to the prince. He looked across the open space of the village to one of the tallest buildings, and saw NeShae's figure in the window, waiting. Then Alex turned his attention to one man who was sitting next to him.

"How are you feeling?" the prince asked the man casually.

"Fine, my prince. And how about yourself?" he replied.

"Just fine," Alex answered and then turned again to the approaching army. He could now make out individual figures and knew that it would not be long. Alex looked to one of the buildings on the other side of the town. He had told the women and young children to stay there with the horses, just in case the worst happened, so they could hopefully ride to safety. The large pots of oil were still boiling over the hot flames that had been built on top of the wall, and Alex could easily see the newly formed catapult in the center of the village. There were three men there, waiting for the signal to fire. Alex only hoped that their quickly built machine would do the job.

The army moved closer, and Alex very carefully searched each and every one of the members, trying to catch a glimpse of his father. He wasn't surprised when he didn't see him, however, for he didn't think that his father and his captor would be in the front ranks. He could see that there was a group of troops that stayed near the rear, in a small cluster of trees, and figured that the king was most likely there. The men on top of the wall were starting to get anxious, as nearly all of them had knocked an arrow ready, waiting for the moment to surprise their unsuspecting rivals. Then they heard, a scream. A high-pitched, hideous scream made by one member in the approaching army. Then another followed, and soon the entire force began their battle cry as they started running, weapons raised, toward the wall. One of the men on the wall started to stand, but James quickly grabbed his shoulder and shook his head no in response. Everyone watched Alex patiently, waiting for his signal. The screaming horde came closer, but still he waited. The men became increasingly uneasy, wondering if the prince were going to ever give the signal. He finally did. In one fluid motion, the prince stood up, pulled on the magical string of his bow, and released it. His arrow snapped into the air and sped directly toward its target. It struck one of the creatures in the chest, and Alex watched as it fell to the ground, motionless. The magical arrow continued, however, and struck the creature behind it, killing it also.

The charging army thought nothing of the one soldier standing on the wall until nearly one hundred others stood up and released a volley of arrows at their victims. The shock of these waiting archers was almost more of a blow to the army than the attack itself, for it sent a few of them running in the opposite direction. The majority of the army of orcs and goblins were experienced, however, and continued on their chosen path of destruction. The archers continued to fire, hoping to slow the creatures down. One of the men standing next to Matthew was struck with a stone that came from one of the goblin's slings, and Matthew watched, horrified, as he fell off the wall, landing on the other side. Matthew actually hoped that he had died, so that he wouldn't have to face the cruelty of the creatures who were only a few hundred yards away from him.

Alex watched and waited as the creatures slowly advanced, knowing that their trench was only few yards in front of them. The first one to hit it fell flat on its face, as did the next five or six. They were stalled, and Alex knew it was time to try the catapult. He yelled down to the men to fire, and they did. A flaming ball of pitch soared right over the heads of the soldiers on the protective wall. The missile nearly hit a portion of the wall and the men on it, but just missed. It was close enough, however, to light one of the men's clothes on fire as it flew by. James immediately jumped on the man and tried to pound out the deadly flames. As he extinguished the last flames, Alex watched as the large flame ball struck the ground, directly behind the largest group of creatures. Alex cursed at the catapult, wishing that it would have hit only a few yards shorter. He yelled down to the men to reload, and then continued firing blindly into the approaching crowd. The prince took a short breather to turn his attention to the man who had been burned by the catapult's missile. He was lying on the platform on top of the wall, screaming in pain. Alex immediately ran over to the man and reached into his backpack. He quickly pulled out one of the healing potions that Artimus had given them and gave it to the man to drink. He gulped down the soothing formula, and within minutes was able to make his way down the wall and into one of the buildings that had been prepared for the wounded. Alex watched as two women helped him into the building, then he turned again and began firing.

A large number of creatures had been wounded in the original surprise attack, but now they had regrouped, and most of them were safely across the man-made trench. They had all drawn their shields and were well protected from most of the incoming arrows—all of them except for Alex's. They pushed on, not wanting to lose any ground, and within less than an hour, they were at the town's closed gate. With them they had brought a large battering ram, and they were preparing to use it on the gate in front of them. It was already starting to get dark, and Alex knew that the sun would be setting soon. He knew that they had to find a way to stop this ramming attempt. He looked around, searching for anything that would help. Something, or someone, rather, caught his attention. It was NeShae. The first hit from the ram struck the gate dead center, shaking the entire structure. NeShae was standing on top of the wall next to a small group of soldiers, with her staff in one hand, while she chanted her power-giving words. The second hit cracked the sturdy wooden gate and sent a few of the men down the ladders on the wall, ready to make a stand if the orcs made their way through the gate.

Then they saw the light. It flashed from NeShae's staff and shot directly at the large wooden ram that was in the hands of over twenty goblins and orcs. The light struck the ram near the middle, and it instantly caught on fire. The flames leapt from the wooden beam, torching everything that dared get in its way, including the twenty or so creatures that had been holding it. Alex looked over to NeShae and smiled as he watched her make her way back down the ladder again.

Although the prince could see that they had killed a fair number of the creatures, the opposing army still outnumbered his own group of novice soldiers. And they weren't the only ones who had taken casualties. As Alex took the time to look around, he could also see that at least twenty of his own men had been injured or killed. For the moment, the remaining creatures had stayed out of arrow's range, regrouping and waiting for the chance to strike again.

Alex rushed over to Matthew to make sure that he was all right. When he saw that he was, he spoke. "I have to get over there." He pointed to the small cluster of trees that hid the rest of the army, and where he thought that his father probably was.

"But how?" Matthew asked, looking at the large number of angry orcs and goblins that stood in his way.

"I'm not sure," Alex said as his eye caught something in the sky. "What's that?" the prince asked Matthew as he pointed to two objects in the quickly darkening sky.

"It's the eagles!" Matthew shouted as he hurried down to the ground. He was met there by NeShae, and they waited for a few moments before the two large birds landed. Most of the eyes in the village were upon them.

NeShae's eyes, however, were still in the sky, searching for something. "Where's the third one?" she whispered only loud enough for herself to hear.

Alex also came down, but told James to watch the monsters carefully. He walked over to NeShae and gave her a smile. "You're responsible for this, aren't you?"

"How'd you ever guess?" she asked him as she returned his grin.

"I've got an idea," Alex said to the group of people surrounding him. "But we have to act fast for it to work."

"What is it?" Matthew asked immediately and listened as Alex explained the entire plan to all of them.

The sun had fully set by now, and only the stars and moon cast any light into the dark night. Both Alex and Matthew climbed onto the animals that they had come to know a few days before, and soon they had taken flight, soaring toward the cluster of trees that Alex had made his target.

The night air was cool, but smoke rose from the various fires that had been started as a result of the battle below. The army of creatures was still motionless as Alex and Matthew flew unnoticed above them. The two companions flew over what appeared to be a large tent set in the center of the clump of trees. Then the second part of the plan began as Alex and Matthew continued to circle the grove of trees.

All of a sudden, the gate in the middle of the giant wall surrounding Danden sprung open, and horses carrying what appeared to be people began fleeing from the enclosed township. The orcs and goblins saw this as a wonderful chance to chase down their confused prey, so they immediately gave their battle cries and ran blindly toward the wall.

Alex and Matthew smiled as they saw the creatures do exactly what Alex had thought they would. They peered carefully down into the darkness, making sure that they could land now without being noticed. When they were sure that they were far enough away from the trees not to be noticed, the eagles made their landing, in about the same place that the army had been just moments before. Alex and Matthew thanked the birds and started off toward the trees and the tent.

Meanwhile, the attacking creatures continued chasing the fleeing horses and what appeared to be riders. They became so involved in catching them that they forgot their positions until one of them actually injured one of the mounts and went over to finish off the riding soldier. It was then that he noticed they were in trouble. As he reached for the head of the rider, he saw that the only thing riding the horse was a large grain sack on top of a wooden stick. Before the creature could shout a warning, an arrow struck him in the throat, killing him instantly. The archers appeared on the wall, firing arrows into the night as the catapult lit up the sky with its blazing spheres.

Alex and Matthew moved quietly through the little brush that surrounded them until they were almost on top of the tent that stood in front of them. They stayed behind a tree, watching what was happening just a few yards away. One very large orc was standing next to a shorter man who was wearing a long robe.

"What do you mean, they attacked again?" the human shouted at the top of his lungs as he struck the orc in the chest with his left fist.

The creature mumbled something that Alex couldn't understand, then walked off toward another small group of orcs off in the distance.

"Dlemar!" the man shouted, directing his voice toward the tent. "Get out here! We're moving!"

Alex couldn't stop himself when he heard his father's name. He immediately grabbed his bow and jumped from the cover of the trees. "Hold it!" he shouted as he aimed one of the magical arrows directly at the stranger.

The man slowly turned around to face this threatening voice. He looked Alex over for quite a long time before finally saying, "So, you finally made it. I was beginning to have doubts, my foolish little prince."

"Shut up!" Alex shouted.

"Touchy, touchy," the robed human said, and he started to walk toward the tent.

"Stop, I said!" Alex yelled as he pulled the magical string on his bow back even farther.

"Whatever you say," the man answered. He stood there for a moment longer before he shouted, "Langwar!" Alex released the string, waiting to see the comforting light of his magical arrow soar through the darkness. But he saw nothing. Not even the tent anymore. Everything was total and complete darkness. No moon, no stars, nothing. He shouted to Matthew, hoping that he would hear his voice, but everything was silent. Darkness and silence. All that Alex could hear was his own heart beating inside of his chest. Then he felt a crushing blow strike his arm as his treasured bow flew from his hands. He was going to go grab it, but he couldn't see where it went.

"Face me like a man, you coward!" Alex shouted, but was shocked when he heard no sound. "I can't get rattled," he said to himself as he thought about the magical spell that had been cast on him. "I have to be calm. Then he felt a searing pain rip through his shoulder as he reached over and felt the handle of a dagger protruding from his body. He reached over with his right hand and jerked the knife from his left shoulder, giving a silenced cry of pain as he did so. Then an image came to him—an image of him and Artimus in the woods. Alex grabbed the sword that was strapped to his back and held it in front of him. Another blow struck him in the face, spilling what felt like blood all over Alex's body. He screamed, more angry at not hearing his anger than anything. "Concentrate," he whispered to himself as he tried to imagine the man's next move. "Concentrate, concentrate," he chanted. Almost on instinct, the prince threw up his sword, and felt the striking of metal as he blocked the oncoming blow. He tried to counter, but found nothing but air. The prince settled back and again tried to put himself in his attacker's shoes, imagining what he would do next, where he would strike. Alex moved his weapon to the side, once again feeling the collision of metal, and once again counterattacking. This time was different, however, for the prince struck something with his blow. Immediately he swung again, hoping that he could hit his target twice, but he felt nothing the second time. The only thing he felt was a metal weapon tear into his leg, making him scream in silence once again. Alex was getting tired, and he knew that he couldn't take much more of this punishment, but he stood still, waiting for the next strike. He could feel this one easily, and he could tell that it was a strike filled with hatred. Alex held his sword crossways above his head, hoping to block any attack coming from that direction. Sure enough, he did. The blow was a powerful one, but Alex kept his poise as he fought to hold the attacker's sword above his head. The deadly weapon came closer, pushing Alex's own weapon nearer and nearer to his body. Alex suddenly dropped his injured left arm, holding his sword with only his right arm, and reached for his boot. He easily found what he was looking for and quickly brought his concealed dagger into the stomach of his opponent. Alex felt the weight of his opponent's weapon disappear, as did the darkness, until he could see clearly again. He was standing over the body of the robed man, who was lying motionless on the ground in front of him. The prince, not wanting to take any chances, quickly raised his sword and drove it deep into the figure's chest.

"Alex, are you all right?" Matthew shouted as he exited the tent with the king.

"Father!" Alex shouted as he slowly dragged his injured body over to his father. Dlemar didn't move, however, and Alex stood there, confused at what was happening. "Father, it's me!" he said again, hoping that the king would come out of his strange trance.

"What's wrong with him?" Matthew asked slowly.

"I don't know, but we've got to get him back to the village." Alex held onto his father's shoulders, trying not to fall on account of his injuries, and trying to get his father's attention.

Matthew immediately began waving to their friends, who had been circling around them the whole time, and within minutes the birds had landed in front of the three men.

"Will he get on one of the birds?" Matthew asked Alex.

"He better, because I'm not carrying him back," Alex answered and listened as Matthew chuckled. the king offered no resistance, but simply did as they told him, not saying a word, and never changing his expression from the blank look that he held. In a very short time, they were once again inside the walls of the city of Danden. James and NeShae ran at once to their sides, helping Alex off of the eagle that had helped them. Alex laid on the ground, watching the blood seep from his wounds. NeShae dug in one of her pockets for a moment before she pulled out a small bottle and put it to Alex's lips. The prince could feel the coolness of the liquid flow through every part of his body until he could easily talk again.

He opened his eyes and looked up. The first person that he saw was James.

"The creatures!" Alex screamed. "We've got to stop…"

"Shhhh, don't worry, my friend," James reassured him. "The ones that aren't dead are still running."

"Good," Alex said as he moved his eyes to another body

that hovered over him.

"Artimus!" he shouted as he sat up straight.

"So you can remember me after all," the old elf's wise voice answered.

"But—but how…" Alex started.

Another very familiar voice interrupted. "Artimus and I came by eagle express as soon as we received word of your trouble."

"Merquilla," Alex stated with a smile. "But how did you know?"

Artimus once again spoke up as he touched the beak of the black falcon that was perched on his right shoulder. "A very wise and dear friend of mine told us."

Alex slowly sat up, wanting to understand everything that was going on around him. "But what about my father? It's like he doesn't even know we're here."

"Which is precisely why we are here, my dear child," Merquilla answered. "The crown that your father wears is the Crown of Vallchem, an evil artifact that is used to control people's minds. We only lately learned of this from Ptilon, Artimus's wonderful animal friend." Merquilla gave Artimus a loving smile and then continued. "By killing the Crown's master, you also killed your father's master. And without someone to tell him what to do, your father remains in this sleepy state."

"But how can we stop this?" Alex asked in a worried tone as NeShae tended to his slowly healing wounds.

"You must get some rest if you're going to get any better," Artimus stated, "but Merquilla and I will try to help your father as much as possible."

"Please, Artimus," Alex pleaded as his eyes started closing from exhaustion. "I need my father back."

"I know," Artimus said and watched as the prince closed his eyes.

"Good morning," NeShae said as she kissed Alex softly on the cheek.

"NeShae!" Alex jumped up out of the bed that he had been moved to the night before. "My father—is he all right?" he asked hesitantly.

"I don't know," NeShae answered him as she stood up and walked back to the doorway that she had entered just a few minutes earlier. "Why don't you ask him yourself?"

The prince's face lit up as he watched his father walk proudly through the door with a smile on his face. Alex couldn't say a word. He stood up and walked over to the man he had been searching for since his journey began. Dlemar grabbed his son in his arms and gave him a strong loving hug as they both shed the tears that had been trying so hard to get out during the last few weeks. They embraced for quite a long time before finally being interrupted by a whole crowd of people. First Artimus came in, followed by NeShae, Merquilla, Matthew, and James.

Alex walked over to Artimus and Merquilla, and gave each of them a warm hug. As Merquilla's eyes filled with tears, Alex spoke softly. "Thank you. I owe you both more than I can ever repay." Then they all made their way outside to where most of the damage had been done. They could plainly see the rubble and debris caused by the army that had attacked only a short time ago. There were still a few bodies lying around, most of them belonging to the enemy, and these were being gathered into the middle of the town so that they could all be burned.

As they stood looking at the area around them, James broke the silence by saying loud enough for the many people around him to hear, "My friends, it has been a long couple of days for us, indeed, and it will be long before the mourning is over, but let us not forget that we have been saved from a destruction that could have been far greater! Let us tonight feast in victory and in thanks to the prince and his companions!"

So that night, food in great quantities was prepared for everyone and set out amidst the scattered rubble of the city for all to eat. Under the moonlight, Alex and NeShae slipped quietly away for a few moments to themselves. They stood quietly, looking at the stars for what seemed like centuries, until Alex finally spoke.

"NeShae," he said.

"Yes," she answered, looking into his eyes.

"Are we still on for that special event that I asked you about before the battle?"

"I wouldn't miss it if a hundred more mages stood in my way. Of course, I would love to be your wife," NeShae answered, and finished by giving the prince a long-overdue hug.

"Well then, my future princess, shall we tell the others the good news?"

"After you, my prince," NeShae answered, and so they decided to walk back and tell the others their news. They made their announcement and gave everyone another reason to celebrate. As they were all standing there, Artimus finally spoke again in a soft, wise tone.

"Well, at least something good has come out of this. At least you two have found each other." They all smiled as their glances turned slowly to Artimus who was examining the object that he held in his hands. It was the Crown, and it was still sparkling as though it were some great treasure meant for wonderful purposes. For a moment they all peered at the Crown, wondering what would happen now, and then slowly, one by one, they turned their attention back to the party—all except for Artimus, who looked up to the sky and saw Ptilon the falcon and another figure, floating gracefully through the air.

Ptilon circled over the town, watching everything from far above. Something else caught his eye, however, and he raced to meet it. He took his eyes away from the city for a moment and turned his attention to his newfound companion. Artimus looked up just in time to see the two falcons soaring high above the trees, together.